THE TEEN

TOOLKIT

Life Skills Not Taught In Schools

KOREN A. NORTON

TABLE OF CONTENTS

Acknowledgements 1

Introduction 3

Chapter 1: 3 Essential Tools to Make It in This World .. 5

Chapter 2: Common Sense and Street Smarts 20

Chapter 3: Dealing with Difficult Emotions 31

Chapter 4: Problem-Solving and Critical Thinking 42

Chapter 5: Having a Mentor 57

Chapter 6: How to Get Along with People? 70

Chapter 7: Financial Literacy: Money 101 81

Chapter 8: How to Make Money? 93

Chapter 9: Stress Management & Self Care 105

Chapter 10: The Art of Negotiation 119

Chapter 11: Setting and Achieving Goals 132

Chapter 12: Choosing a Career 141

Chapter 13: Building Self-Confidence..........................152

Chapter 14: Handling Conflict.....................................163

Chapter 15: Managing Your Digital Presence 179

Chapter 16: How to Be a Model Citizen 188

Conclusion 200

About the Author 202

ACKNOWLEDGEMENTS

First and foremost, I want to express my heartfelt gratitude to the incredible young people in my life. Your energy, curiosity, and passion inspire me every day. Thank you for sharing your stories, insights, and dreams with me. This book is dedicated to you, and I hope it empowers you to reach for the stars and make your mark on the world.

I would also like to extend my deepest appreciation to Dr. Elijah James, whose expertise, guidance, and unwavering support were instrumental in shaping this book. Your keen eye for detail and commitment to excellence have truly made a difference, and I am immensely grateful for your collaboration.

A special 'Thank You' to you, Ancier White, for your invaluable assistance throughout the writing and editing process. Your dedication, enthusiasm, and hard work have been indispensable, and I could not have completed this project without you.

To all the mentors, educators, and advocates who continue to champion the next generation, thank you for your tireless efforts and unwavering belief in the potential of youth. Your support is invaluable and deeply appreciated.

INTRODUCTION

Hey there! Welcome to your go-to guide for conquering the real world. As you gear up to tackle life beyond the classroom, we know you've got questions – and we've got answers. From managing money to mastering relationships and everything in between, we're here to help you navigate adulthood like a pro.

There is so much you didn't cover in school and we have addressed some of these issues for you. In these pages, you'll find down-to-earth advice and real-life stories to guide you through life's ups and downs. Whether you're figuring out how to budget, acing that job interview, or figuring out the world of friendships and dating, we've got your back.

So, get ready to dive in, learn some new skills, and discover how to thrive in today's fast-paced world. Let's tackle this adventure together because you've got what it takes to succeed.

Chapter 1

3 Essential Tools to Make It in This World

There was a girl named Liz Murray whose parents were both drug addicts. As a child, when the government support checks came, her parents would buy drugs first and then buy 

food with what was left. Liz and her sister would eat ice or toothpaste when hungry as they often went without food. Liz's mom died from AIDS. She had become HIV positive because she was sharing needles with other addicts. Later, on, her Dad also would sadly, die of AIDS. Eventually, Liz became homeless and hopeless. She eventually enrolled back into High School and submitted an essay to get a scholarship to attend Harvard University, one of the most prestigious universities in the United States.

You can imagine her excitement when she was accepted. Liz's story was made into a movie called "From Homeless to Harvard". If Liz could have made it despite all her circumstances, you can too!!!

Maybe you have parents who are addicts
Maybe you have experimented with drugs
Maybe you were compared to your siblings as a child
Maybe you were bullied because you were darker than others, bigger than others or you were a migrant
Maybe someone called you no good
Maybe you were told you wouldn't amount to anything
In spite of all that, you can make it in this world.
Three characteristics can make a difference for you.

Resilience
Grit
Perseverance

Some of us when we were growing up, had many dreams. One of my young friend's first fantasies was to be an astronaut, which may sound strange for a Caribbean teenager. He thought that if he worked hard and did well in physics, he would make it.

But then he began reading al

l of the conditions for him to do so, and he realized it was more than what he wanted to do and the odds were too slim. He started reading several books and looking at the reality of life in his country, he decided he could do more good by becoming a doctor. Now, he is happy with his decision. It was not easy working through medical school, but he succeeded.

What do you need to make in this world?

Resilience

Grit

Perseverance

I tell you, it's not always going to be easy, but it will never stop being an adventure until you give up.

Life is a trip, and the journey becomes easier if you have the right things in your bag... a passport, a ticket, and a destination in mind.

So if you want to make it in life, you have to know where you want to end up. Otherwise, how do you know what direction you should take? And when you start moving in that direction of your dreams and passions, you will reach those obstacles and mountains and roadblocks and speedbumps, but do you stop? No, you pause, but you keep going with your three companions.

Resilience

Grit

Perseverance

You have to train your mind to withstand hardships and obstacles. You have to always hold on to your passion and keep your dreams in sight.

What do you want to do right now, at this particular moment? When you figure it out, you will know what your destination is. Of course, you can change it sometimes, but have something that you are reaching for that means a lot to you.

What do you really desire? What's that precious thing you want to get? Ask your heart and then let your mind listen.

When you decide what that dream or goal is, then you figure out what you need to do to get there. The next step is finding the resources you have that will help you and what you need to ask for help.

What Do You Need To Ask Yourself?

This is a question that everyone must answer, and it will lead us all differently based on what we want out of life. You still have a lot of uncertainty in your life. You are young and eager to learn, eager to get up and make a difference in your own life, and eager to persevere.

I think that once you have an answer to that question you have to ask yourself another thing; am I going to make the world a better place? Determining what you want to do in your life and what impact you want to make are important.

Being a better person entails making your home, your community, your country, or the world a better place for everybody.

Resilience, Grit, and Perseverance: Guiding You

Resilience, Grit, and Perseverance are three of the best companions you can carry with you on your journey of life to achieve the goals you envision for yourself.

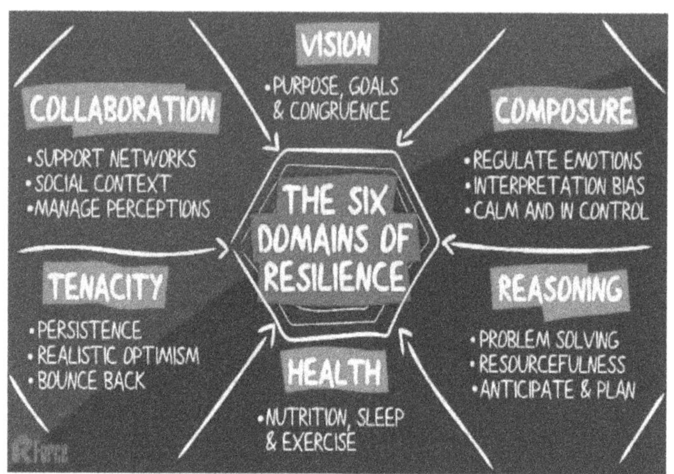

Resilience is the capacity to heal, bounce back, or rebuild from challenges in your experience. It's all about being able to navigate and adjust to a situation, or tension, and yet continue to plough along. Often, you have a stamina that helps you to heal better than others and get back to living life to the fullest or chasing your goal.

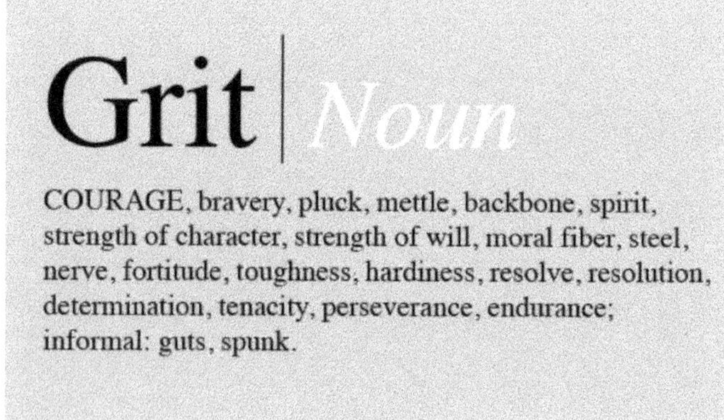

Grit is all about perseverance in pursuit of long-term targets. It all comes down to self-control and the ability to forego immediate pleasure. To me, it's a subtle distinction from perseverance, which necessitates grit in order to endure and persevere.

Perseverance means holding the course and not giving up. You 'persist' – you keep pushing to the finish line no matter how many challenges, hurdles, or delays you encounter on the way to reaching your aspirations or ambitions! To persevere requires having a "never-say-die" attitude, no matter how difficult circumstances are.

I hear you when you say: it is easier said than done. When the people in your own home, like your parents, are ready to give up, how do you push through? Sometimes you feel so alone and as if no one understands. Don't give up though, especially if the goal you are trying to achieve is a good one. You can pause to rest or ask for help, but keep going.

It Couldn't Be Done

BY EDGAR ALBERT GUEST

Somebody said that it couldn't be done
But he with a chuckle replied
That "maybe it couldn't," but he would be one
Who wouldn't say so till he'd tried.
So he buckled right in with the trace of a grin
On his face. If he worried he hid it.
He started to sing as he tackled the thing
That couldn't be done, and he did it!

Remember Usain Bolt? This sprinter from Jamaica started training so young and it wasn't always easy but he persevered until he reached victory.

Your victory might not be as big and as public or as lucrative financially, but it will still make you feel proud to achieve your goal. And every time you achieve a goal, it becomes easier for you to reach for something else because the motivation inside of you builds.

Remember, perseverance builds character!!!
See It Through

By Edgar Albert Guest

When you're up against a trouble,

Meet it squarely, face to face;

Lift your chin and set your shoulders,

Plant your feet and take a brace.

When it's vain to try to dodge it,

Do the best that you can do;

You may fail, but you may conquer,

See it through!

Black may be the clouds about you

And your future may seem grim,

But don't let your nerve desert you;

Keep yourself in fighting trim.

If the worst is bound to happen,

Spite of all that you can do,

Running from it will not save you,

See it through!

Even hope may seem but futile,

When with troubles you're beset,

But remember you are facing

Just what other men have met.

You may fail, but fall still fighting;
Don't give up, whate'er you do;
Eyes front, head high to the finish.
See it through!

Take what Charles Darwin, one of the most important scientists of all time, said: "it is not the strongest of the species that survive, not the most intelligent, but the most responsive to change." There is so much wisdom in those words.

To have the right mindset is key to change and to succeed.

In order to have the right mindset you have to be inspired. Inspiration helps you to feel compelled to action. The drive to work or fight for a cause or the pressures to take advantage of a presented opportunity encourages us to act or think. In this context, motivation is characterized as an internal disposition that drives a person toward a desired end-state where the motive is met, and a target is defined as the representation of the desired outcome that an individual has.

You Need to Learn From Your Mistakes

No one is resistant to making mistakes – we are, after all, human! However, if we just apologize and move on as before, we risk making the same mistakes.

We cause undue burden on others and ourselves because we do not learn from our mistakes, and we risk losing people's respect and trust in us.

How you see your errors influences how you respond to them and what you do next. Chances are, you'll remember your mistake in a bad way for as long as the initial shock and pain last and you know sometimes others don't let you forget it, as they keep throwing it back in your face, even when you have moved past it.

However, reframe the mistake as a learning opportunity and you can inspire yourself to become better based on your experiences; you now have a better idea of what works, what doesn't and what not to do.

The ability to bounce back and be resilient will come in handy when you make a mistake or fall. The harder you throw a ball, the higher it bounces back up. Think about that.

Start To Believe 10000% in You

"Belief" is one of the characteristics of an optimistic outlook. Believing in your ability helps you transcend negative feelings and labels placed on you by others, such as "you'll never amount to anything". The persons who said that to you might not even have believed it as he or she might have just been speaking out of anger or frustration. What is most important is that you should not believe it. What gives them the right to think that they can determine your future and the quality of your life just based on their limited perceptions?

You have to believe in yourself more than anyone else does and move in the direction of your best dreams.

Do you trust yourself and your abilities? Are you besieged by fear and self-doubt? That's normal. There is a book that is called, "Feel the fear and do it anyway". Self-doubt will creep up but just keep practicing what it is you want to get good at and keep putting one foot in front of the other.

Think of Grit as that drive in you that keeps you going... that hunger for better, that thing that helps you to keep sending in scholarship applications because you want to get a degree and your parents have no money, that quality that makes you call back an employer time and time again because you want a job.

Maybe you deserve good things, but life doesn't always just hand them to us... we have to keep at it.

You might look at others and think that they have it easy or something comes naturally to them. I won't deny it that playing a musical instrument, doing math, cooking, designing clothes or playing a sport might seem to come naturally to some persons. But you know what studies have found? A person who practices something for about 10,000 hours can become an expert at it. Practice, practice, practice... take action. Talent alone is not enough. Dogged determination is the thing!!!

Resilience

Grit

Perseverance

Keep going even when you want to give up and when you fall, don't stay there. Get. Right. Back. Up!!!

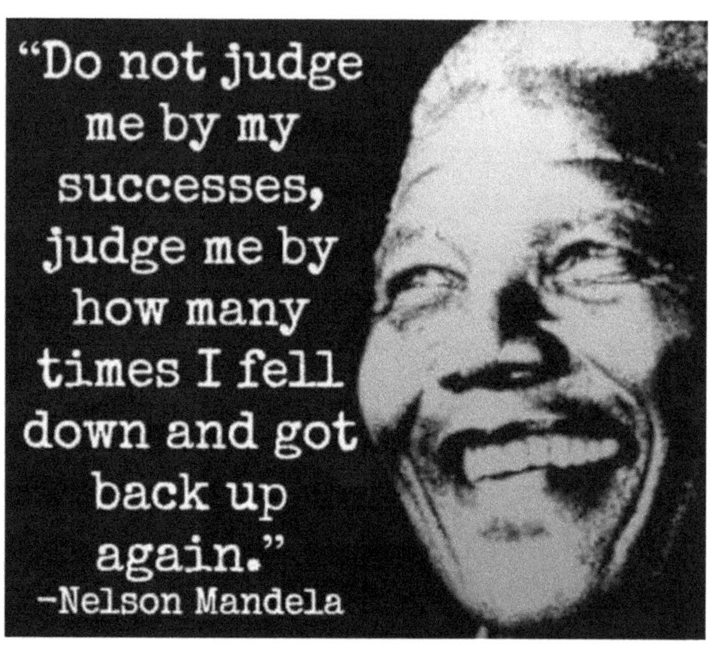

In conclusion, I believe that resilience, grit and perseverance are three incredibly important tools that should become your new friends. You need to ask yourself the most important question: "What do I really want?" and am I willing to go the distance to get it.

When you can step out into the world boldly, knowing that you have a destination in mind and you are determined to reach that goal come what may, you will be as happy as SpongeBob SquarePants as the sun sets. Isn't it what we're all looking for?

Extra Credit: 5 things to Remember

1. Always have your destination (goal) in mind
2. Remember the positive success stories of others
3. Don't listen to the wrong people who are negative
4. Be aware of the possible pitfalls that could come up
5. Stay focused and ask for help when needed

Chapter 2

COMMON SENSE AND STREET SMARTS

Sara is an 18-year-old student who is very active on social media. One Saturday night, when scrolling through her social media app, she noticed a friend request from a stranger and the photo looked like a much older male. Instead of immediately accepting the request, she decided to apply common sense and did the following instead:

- She assessed the situation. She knew that people are strangers until they become friends, but connecting inappropriately with someone she doesn't know could lead to privacy issues, scams, or some other malicious intent.

- She did some information gathering. To make an informed decision, she looked at the person's profile and checked to see if he had any friends in common with her, shared interests or any information that could speak to who the person was. The profile had limited information and they had no friends or interests in common.

- She trusted her instincts. Sara followed her gut feeling which told her that accepting this person as a friend would cause him to see her personal information, and have access to her friends; that made her uncomfortable. She decided to be cautious and protect her online presence.

- She took action: Sara declined the friend request. She believed it was better to prioritize her safety and privacy by connecting only with people she knew and trusted, unless the persons were introduced by a friend, sent a note of introduction with the request, or she could tell clearly who it was.

As you approach adulthood, you will encounter various situations that require common sense and even street smarts to help you navigate life with confidence. These are not things you typically learn in a textbook.

Common sense is described as practical wisdom or the ability to make certain judgements. It is generally developed based on everyday knowledge and through life experiences and not by following a certain training. It can be easily practiced by becoming aware of and reflecting on situations before making decisions. As you develop your common sense, you will be able to make smarter choices.

Here are a few key aspects of common sense:

How do you practice Common Sense in Everyday Living?

How do you live as a youth in this world with so many decisions to make? The answer is, by using common sense to guide your actions and decisions so that you make sensible choices with little to no negative consequences. Whether you are at home, in college, out at a party, on a basketball or volleyball court, or at a job, the need for decision making or quick action can pop up.

Now, you might be wondering how to cultivate and apply common sense in your own life. Here are a few key principles to consider:

- Seek Different Viewpoints: Common sense isn't just about your own understanding; it also involves considering different perspectives. Take the time to listen to others, seek advice, and gather different opinions. This broader view allows you to make more well-rounded decisions that take into account various factors and viewpoints. Make sure the persons you listen to have demonstrated their ability to make wise decisions and sound judgment.
- Learn from Experience: Life is a continuous learning journey, and common sense is developed

through experience- that's why some parents allow their children to touch fire – when they realize it burns, they don't touch it again. Embrace every opportunity to learn and grow, even from your mistakes. Reflect on past experiences and even the experiences of others that you have seen, and use them as valuable lessons to guide your future actions.

- Apply Critical Thinking: Challenge assumptions; for example, just because it was done for 10 years doesn't mean it is the only course of action. Also, stay away from stereotyping.... All women are this or all men are that..., etc. Ask questions, and evaluate information critically. In a world filled with misinformation and biases, having the ability to think critically is essential. This means examining evidence, seeking reliable sources, and questioning ideas and beliefs. It is not disrespectful to ask an adult, even a pastor or a politician to explain something further.

- Practice being practical: Common sense is all about practicality. It is not a "pie in the sky" concept. Something cannot only just sound good, it must make sense. It's about finding simple and effective solutions to everyday problems. Embrace a practical mindset that focuses on what works and what makes sense in real-life situations.

Now to some other good stuff.... **Street smarts...**

What are some possible definitions?

Cambridge dictionary says: The ability to manage or succeed in difficult or dangerous situations, especially in big towns or cities.

Dictionary.com says: Shrewd awareness of how to survive or succeed in any situation, especially as a result of living or working in a difficult environment, as a city ghetto neighbourhood

Based on these definitions we can say that 'street smarts' is practical knowledge you get through personal experience, an understanding of people and the reality of the world around you. It means you have to be aware of your surroundings, being able to adapt to wherever you are and know how to react should something unexpected happen.

How do you develop street smarts?

♦ First and foremost, try as much as possible to stay safe. If you are going somewhere different, notify someone, make sure your phone is charged and keep your eyes open and stay as alert as possible

♦ Be aware of your soundings. Pay attention to your environment, look out for risky situations and be mindful of any potential danger. If you are walking into an area with gangs that are prone to violence, then try not to go alone.

♦ Learn to read people. Observe the body language and facial expressions of the people around you as this might give a clue as to their motives. Pay attention to the social dynamics (if the atmosphere is tense or angry), and make a judgment call if to stay or leave to protect yourself from potential harm.

♦ Awareness of Surroundings: Pay attention to your environment, especially in unfamiliar or potentially risky situations. Stay alert, trust your instincts, and be mindful of potential dangers or opportunities.

Now, let's explore some ***practical*** scenarios where common sense and street smarts come into play:

<u>Personal Safety</u>: Walking alone at night, using public transportation, or exploring new neighborhoods require a combination of common sense and street smarts. Trust your instincts, stick to well-lit areas, and be aware of your surroundings to ensure your personal safety.

<u>Financial Decisions</u>: You barely have an allowance or you get paid in a new job and often what you get is not enough to meet all your needs. I know phone accessories and hair products cost a lot...LOL. When managing money, common sense guides you to save, budget, and make wise decisions on what you need now, what you can get from your parents, and what can wait until later. Street smarts

help you recognize potential scams, avoid impulsive spending, and make informed financial choices.

<u>Social Media and Online Interactions</u>: I know most of you conduct a lot of your interactions on social media... Instagram, TikTok, WhatsApp, etc. Common sense is important for protecting your privacy, avoiding online scams, and using social media responsibly. Street smarts help you differentiate between genuine connections and potential risks, avoiding cyberbullying and just knowing what sites to avoid.

Here are some quick things to remember:

- Think fast on your feet
- Build your self-confidence
- Be resourceful – use what is available
- Don't make yourself a target when you are out
- Learn self-defense skills
- Be observant
- Align yourself with the right persons
- Learn as much as you can
- When all else fails…. Run as fast as you can

Conclusion

Smart young people like I know you are will take this discussion seriously. Street smarts are not an alternative to book smarts- clearly, you need to focus on your studies and learn as much as you can formally. However, so much about life is not taught in the traditional schools and developing common sense and street smarts is a lifelong journey. People who embrace these characteristics tend to have good survival, emotional and social skills.

Remember, common sense and street smarts are not about being overly cautious or distrusting, but about developing practical wisdom and an understanding of the world around you.

Extra Credit: 5 things to Remember

1. If you have a gut feeling about something, get more information before you make a decision.
2. Using common sense helps you to consider whether certain decisions align with your goals and values.
3. Sometimes walking away is the best thing you can do in an unsafe situation
4. Don't do things that are obviously bad for you, or wrong like breaking the law.

5. Just because the majority of people around you are doing something, that does not mean it is right or okay.

Chapter 3

DEALING WITH DIFFICULT EMOTIONS

Alex was 20 years old when his grandmother died. He was heartbroken as she had always been a source of unconditional love and support in his life. They had a lot of memories of laughing  as he teased her about the old soap operas she watched and the cooking shows and she teased him because of the kind of girls he liked and because she said those cooking shows ideas were what fed him so well. She also would give him good advice and he always felt as if she understood him more than his parents.

He had moved away from home for just 3 months when he got the news and he felt overwhelmed with a range of emotions. He felt a deep sense of loss and emptiness, he felt guilty that he had left her and he even felt angry at his parents and her doctor because he wondered if they had done enough to help her. His feelings would change like a roller coaster.

Grief and loss is only one difficult emotion that young people face. Sometimes you have heartbreak after a relationship ends, intense anger at being treated unfairly, frustration at being misunderstood or crushing disappointment when others, parents included, don't live up to expectations or when a promise is broken.

It's common for a young adult to be so overwhelmed with these emotions that it can lead to bouts of depression, anxiety, stress, loneliness or fear as they transition into adulthood.

If you're a young adult who struggles with difficult emotions on a regular basis, it can become exhausting. You might feel like your life is a constant battle between your head and heart and that no one understands you. The good thing is that you have the power to do something about your emotions and make changes in your life.

The road ahead may be filled with obstacles but it doesn't have to be so difficult if you know how to cope with these emotions.

Question for you: Are you a confident, independent young person who's ready to take on the world? Or do you feel scared, anxious, and confused about what comes next? If it's the latter, you're not alone. Many people your age feel this way. That's why we are having this conversation.

- ◆ *Watching the boy you like be with someone else*
- ◆ *Knowing your best friend's father abuses her*
- ◆ *Being worried about the bullies in your community*
- ◆ *Watching your mom struggle with money as a single parent*
- ◆ *Being frustrated that you don't know what next to do with your life*

There are so many things that could be affecting you emotionally right now.

It can be an unsettling time as you leave high school and try to figure out what's next... you might want one thing, your parents another and your friends might be suggesting something else. Do you do some more classes, start college or university or get a job and try to get out of your parent's home as quickly as possible?

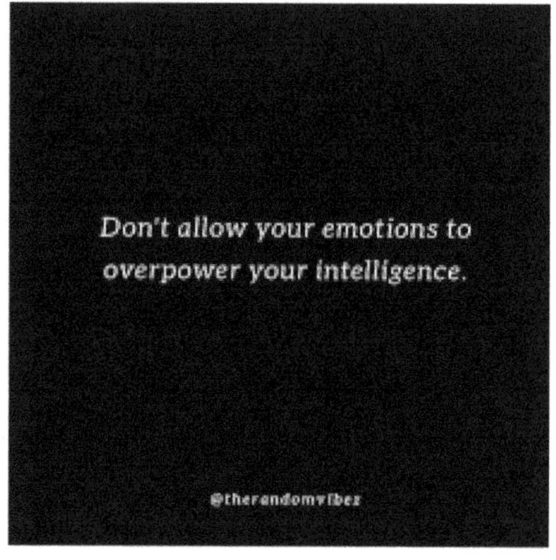

You may be feeling anxious because of all these decision and big changes in your life. For those of you in your late teens, transitioning into adulthood can be challenging. This can be even more true if you're leaving home for the first time, adjusting from living with your parents to living independently and adjusting to life without the structure of high school or home. Making this transition can also bring up a lot of different emotions. At times you may feel excited about your future and other times you may feel scared, unsure or anxious about what lies ahead.

This chapter provides information on how to deal with common negative emotions that many young persons experience after graduating high school, such as fear, self-doubt, anxiety, anger, grief, stress, loneliness, frustration and even depression. Let's look at some practical examples:

Acknowledge and Accept Your Emotions

The first step in dealing with difficult emotions is acknowledging and accepting them. Sometimes we want to fight as if we should not have negative emotions, but we are human. It is not a sign of anything being wrong with you, it's normal and okay to feel a wide range of emotions. Give yourself permission to experience and express these emotions without judgment or self-criticism. By accepting your emotions, you open the door to understanding their underlying causes and finding healthy ways to address them.

Practice Self-Care

Self-care plays an important role in managing difficult emotions. Engage in activities that bring you joy and help you relax. This may include hobbies, exercise, spending time in nature, journaling, or connecting with loved ones. Prioritize your well-being by getting enough sleep, eating healthy food, and maintaining a balanced lifestyle. Remember, taking care of yourself is not selfish; it's a necessary part of managing and coping with difficult emotions. Bear in mind that limited sleep, being hungry or overusing too much violent video games can affect your mood and emotional state.

Get support

It's important to remember that you don't have to face difficult emotions alone. Reach out to trusted friends, family members, or mentors who can provide a listening ear and offer guidance. You might have a favorite teacher, an aunt that you get along with or even consider talking to a counselor who can provide professional support. For some teens, an online support group is also helpful.

Develop Appropriate Coping Techniques

We already said it's normal to feel difficult emotions and it's okay to ask for help. What I don't want you to do is to react in ways that could make you feel worse like hitting something, cutting yourself or smoking. What is better is to engage in activities that help you process and express your emotions, such as listening to music, writing in a journal, creating art, working out at a gym or home, playing sports or looking at positive Instagram or TikTok videos. Find healthy outlets that allow you to release tension and channel your emotions in a good way.

Cultivate Resilience

Resilience is the ability to bounce back from difficult experiences – you might have done it without even giving it a name. When you got a D and you worked hard to still pass the class, when you lost your dog and managed to work through the grief, when you had someone gossip about you and you didn't want to go to school, but you held your head high and went. Resilience is about recognizing that setbacks and challenges are opportunities for learning and growth. Cultivate resilience by answering negative thoughts with positive ones (replace I'm a failure with I will do better next time). It's also good to think about solutions to problems instead of just lingering on the problem.

Pause before you act

Don't make any major decisions when you are overwhelmingly stressed or angry because you might impulsively do the wrong thing and get into trouble. Walk away from a fight, put the phone in another room for 15 minutes so you don't get the urge to send harmful or hurtful texts or just take some deep breaths until you feel calm. Actually, another thing that works is getting a cold ice cube and holding it for as long as you can; its distracting and can temporarily take your mind off a situation to give you time to develop a more long-term plan.

Focus on what makes you happy

Sometimes when you are grieving or angry or things are not going your way, focus on doing or enjoying something that makes you happy What do you love to do? What do you enjoy? Think about all of the things that you've enjoyed throughout your life and try to incorporate those things into your daily routine. You may want to get involved in a hobby or art project, or you may want to volunteer to help others. The more you focus on what makes you happy, the less time you will spend thinking about the things that are challenging you right now. You have the right to feel happy, positive, and optimistic during this time in your life. And the more you focus on things that make you happy, the closer you will be to living a life that you love.

Remember we talked about Alex who lost his grandmother? Alex decided to honour his grandmother's memory by collecting photos of her and keeping them on his phone. He wrote a goodbye letter and he vowed that he would do well at college because it's what she would have wanted and he knew she would have been proud of him.

Over time, as Alex continued to actively engage in his healing process, he experienced a gradual shift in his emotions. While the pain of loss remained, he learned to honor his grandmother's memory, found solace in shared stories, and gradually reached a sense of acceptance. Though challenging, this journey helped Alex grow stronger and more resilient, ultimately shaping his character and his ability to cope with future difficult emotions.

Reminders:

- Don't blame others for your emotions. It is how you feel as a reaction to something you are experiencing.
- Many of the emotions you feel are temporary

- Learn not to allow other people to control your emotions. People will provoke you or be mean, but you can choose to ignore them.

Conclusion

Dealing with difficult emotions is an essential part of your journey as a youth. It can be challenging, but it can also be a great opportunity to grow and to discover new things about yourself. By acknowledging and accepting your emotions, developing emotional awareness, practicing self-care, seeking support, and cultivating healthy coping mechanisms and resilience, you can navigate the stormy seas of difficult emotions with greater ease and resilience.

Remember, it's okay to ask for help and take time for yourself. Embrace your emotions as valuable messengers, guiding you toward self-discovery, personal growth, and emotional well-being. Later on, you will look back on this time in your life and see how it shaped and prepared you for the future. You have the power to get through this and come out on the other side a stronger, wiser and more confident person.

You've got this!

Extra Credit: 5 things to Remember

1. Everyone feels difficult emotions, so it is normal to feel these things sometimes

2. You have to learn about yourself and figure out what makes you feel calm and relaxed so you can use these techniques to cope with stress, anger or frustration.

3. Always pause before you act so you don't do something that you will regret later on.

4. It's always helpful to talk to someone you trust, who will listen to you and give you good advice. It could be a friend or a professional counselor.

5. Every time you overcome a difficult emotion, you become stronger and better able to deal with what life brings.

Chapter 4

PROBLEM-SOLVING AND CRITICAL THINKING

Once upon a time in the bustling town of Rivertown, there lived a 16-year-old named Jake. One day, Jake found himself in a tight spot when he forgot his house keys. Frustrated and impatient, 

he decided to climb through an open window, thinking it would be a quick solution.

However, his plan backfired when a neighbor spotted him and, unaware of Jake's innocent intentions, reported a potential break-in. Soon, the police arrived, and Jake found himself in a situation he never imagined.

If only Jake had taken a moment to consider alternative solutions, like calling his parents or seeking help from a neighbor, he could have avoided the misunderstanding. This experience taught Jake the importance of good problem-solving skills and thinking through consequences before acting.

Problem-solving is like a superpower humans have. We use our brains to figure out solutions to all kinds of problems, whether they're big and complicated or small and simple. This skill is so important for success in different parts of life, like school and work. It involves thinking hard, being creative, and bouncing back when things get tough.

So, what is problem-solving exactly? Well, it's like being a detective. First, you find a problem; then, you break it down into smaller pieces to understand it better. After that, you come up with smart plans to fix the problem or make it better. This way of thinking isn't just for school subjects; it's useful in science, business, and even when dealing with friends and family.

In science, researchers use the scientific method to solve problems. They make educated guesses, run experiments, and learn from what they observe. In business, bosses and business owners face all sorts of challenges, like changes in the market or problems within the company. They use their brains to come up with smart ideas to overcome these challenges and make things better.

Young people like you would tend to ask friends or use Google or social media to find solutions to problems. It helps to see how someone just like you is solving their problems.

Problem-solving is like a secret weapon we all have. It helps us do well in school, work, and life in general. And the cool thing is, the more we practice, the better we become at finding awesome solutions to all kinds of problems!

Being creative is another big part of solving problems. It's about thinking in new and different ways, coming up with fresh ideas, and being open to trying new stuff. While critical thinking helps you understand problems, creativity helps you find cool and innovative solutions. When you mix critical thinking and creativity, it's like having a superpower for solving problems. This is why it's awesome to encourage creativity in schools and workplaces so that people feel free to think outside the box and come up with amazing ideas.

Being able to adapt is like being a problem-solving superhero. In our fast-changing world, problems sometimes change; they can change and grow. So, being adaptable means you can change your plans when needed, come up with new strategies, and be flexible in your thinking and actions. This is super important because it helps you face unexpected challenges and take advantage of new opportunities. Being adaptable is like knowing that things can change and you're ready to handle whatever comes your way.

Resilience means being strong and not giving up when things get tough. When we try to solve problems, we might face difficulties and make mistakes. Resilience is like having the courage to keep going, learn from our mistakes, and find new ways to solve problems. It helps us stay determined and overcome challenges instead of seeing them as impossible obstacles. Resilience is like a superpower that keeps us moving forward.

Problem-solving isn't just something we do alone – it's also a team effort where people from different backgrounds and cultures come together. When we work as a team, we can use everyone's strengths and ideas to come up with creative solutions. In areas like engineering and making new products, teams with diverse skills can tackle complicated problems. This mix of different viewpoints helps us find complete solutions that consider all aspects.

Technology has brought exciting changes to how we solve problems. Computers and artificial intelligence (AI) help us analyze huge amounts of information and find patterns we might miss. Machine learning, a type of AI, can predict outcomes and improve solutions, especially in complex situations. But, it's essential to use technology responsibly. We must think about ethical issues, like making sure our solutions are fair and don't invade people's privacy.

Even though technology is powerful, it can't replace the important role humans play in problem-solving – so asking an aunt, a friend or a teacher for guidance and advise is still useful. We need to make sure our solutions follow ethical guidelines, meaning they match what society thinks is right. Ethical problem-solving considers everyone, includes different perspectives and doesn't create more problems or inequalities. It's about finding solutions that are good for everyone and don't cause harm.

Critical thinking is like a superpower for your brain. It helps you think carefully and make smart decisions. Instead of just accepting things you hear or read, critical thinking makes you question and really understand what's going on. It's not about memorizing facts; it's about being a detective for information.

Imagine you have a detective hat on, and your job is to figure out the truth. One important part of this superpower is looking at information without letting your feelings or opinions get in the way. It would help if you were like a robot, neutral and open-minded. This helps you figure out if something is true or not. Critical thinkers are really good at telling the difference between facts (true things) and opinions (what someone thinks).

Another cool thing about critical thinking is that it encourages you to challenge what you think you know. Instead of just believing something because everyone else does, critical thinkers like to explore different ideas. They know that everyone has their way of seeing things, and they want to learn from as many different perspectives as possible. This helps make our world more understanding and open-minded.

Critical thinking is like having a detective brain that helps you understand things better, make good choices, and be open to different ideas. It's a superpower that makes you smarter and helps make the world a better place.

Albert Einstein said, "we cannot solve problems with the same thinking we sued to create them.

Problem-Solving and Critical Thinking

When it comes to solving problems, critical thinking is super important. It means taking big problems and breaking them into smaller parts. Critical thinkers are good at understanding how these parts relate to each other and coming up with creative solutions. Instead of just dealing with the symptoms of a problem, they focus on the root causes, making it easier to solve challenges.

Critical Thinking in School

Schools know how important it is for students to be good critical thinkers. That's why the things you learn in class aren't just facts; they also help you learn how to analyze and solve problems. Teachers organize activities and discussions to encourage you to think really carefully about what you're learning. This helps you not only do well in school but also prepares you for dealing with tricky situations in the real world.

Critical Thinking and Communication

Being able to think critically also helps you communicate better. If you can think clearly, you can explain your ideas well, back up your arguments with proof, and have meaningful conversations. This is super important in a world where being able to communicate effectively is crucial for success in many different areas. So, thinking critically doesn't just help you understand things better; it also helps you express your ideas in a way that makes a big impact.

Workplace Skills

Right now, maybe you are in college, at home or even have a part time job. When you work at a job, bosses really like it when you're good at thinking carefully about things. This is because jobs are always changing, and there are lots of new things happening in the world. People who are good at critical thinking can help solve problems and come up with new and cool ideas at work. They can handle tough situations and keep going even when things are tricky. Critical thinkers are also really good at bringing in new ways of looking at things and making the workplace better all the time. For the boss, this means he or she doesn't have to be looking over your shoulder all the time because they know you will be able to use your judgement or think on your feet.

Learning to Think Critically

Being a good critical thinker isn't something you're born with; you learn it over time. Schools, employers and you all have a part to play in getting better at critical thinking. There are some tricks and habits you can use to get better at it, like asking questions that make you think a lot (they call this Socratic questioning), talking a lot in class or with friends, and solving real-life problems. These things help you become a better critical thinker.

Decision-making is something we all do every day, from picking what to wear to making big choices in our lives. It's like a way of figuring out what we should do to get what we want. The choices we make affect how happy we are, how well we do in our jobs, and how successful a group or organization is. To make good decisions, it's important to understand how the process works and what factors play a role in it.

When we make decisions, our brains go through different steps. First, we notice there's a problem or a choice to be made. Then, we gather information about our options. After that, we think about each option and decide which one is the best for what we want. This whole process is called the cognitive process, and it's crucial to understand how it works.

Making decisions can be simple, like choosing what to have for breakfast, or it can be not very easy, like deciding what career to pursue. For simple choices, we often rely on habits and what we usually do without thinking too much. But for big decisions, we need to think carefully about all the different factors before choosing the best option. It's like playing a game where you have to think about all the moves before making the best one. Understanding how decisions work helps us make better choices in our lives.

Decision-making involves a mix of things that happen inside our heads and stuff that's going on around us. Let's talk about the things inside our heads first. There are some sneaky things called cognitive biases, which are like our brains playing tricks on us. They can make us see things a certain way, even if it's not the best way. Emotions also join the decision-making party – sometimes, they help, and other times, they can make things a bit messy. For example, feeling scared might make us avoid risks while being super excited could make us take more risks. Knowing about these tricks and feelings is important so we can make better decisions.

Let's step outside our heads and look at what's happening around us. The environment, or what's going on in the world, can affect our decisions, too. Imagine trying to decide something when you're in a big hurry or when there's not much information available – that can be tough! Stress can also crash the decision-making party and make it harder for us to think clearly. So, figuring out how to handle these outside things is key to making good decisions.

When we're making decisions with a group of people, like in a team or at school, it gets even more interesting. Everyone in the group has their ideas and ways of thinking. Sometimes, though, everyone wants to agree so much that they stop thinking for themselves – that's called groupthink, and it can lead to not-so-great decisions. Making sure everyone talks openly and values different opinions helps the group make smart choices together.

Whether we're making decisions by ourselves or with friends, understanding how our minds work and paying attention to what's happening around us helps us make the best choices.

In today's world, technology plays a big role in helping people make decisions. There are special tools like big data analytics, artificial intelligence, and machine learning that organizations use to make better choices. These tools can quickly look at a lot of information, find patterns, and give helpful insights. But, relying too much on technology brings some problems, like keeping people's information private, biases in computer programs, and the need for humans to understand and explain the results. It's important to find the right balance between human thinking and using technology to get the most benefits.

When making decisions, it's crucial to think about what is right and fair. Decisions can affect not just the immediate result but also people, communities, and even whole societies. Ethical decision-making means looking at choices and thinking about how they will affect different groups of people. Organizations are realizing that making ethical decisions is important not just because it's the right thing to do, but also to build trust and keep a good reputation.

Some decisions are really important and happen at the highest levels of organizations. These are called strategic decisions, and they shape the overall direction of a company. If you are planning to go into business, you will need to learn more about strategic thinking. People making strategic decisions have to deal with uncertainty, think about future challenges, and make sure the company's resources match its long-term goals. This process is always changing, with constant monitoring and adjusting to new situations.

Decision-making isn't just for individuals and organizations; it also happens on a larger scale in societies and governments. People who make policies face challenges because they have to balance the different needs and wants of a whole population. Political, economic, and social factors all play a part in deciding what's best for everyone. Good governance means making decisions in a way that's clear and includes the opinions of many different people.

So I know this was a lot to chew on but it's really important for you to know these things and trust me...just by reading this chapter and putting your brain to work will take you way ahead of most youth your age.

Extra Credit: 5 Things to Remember

1. Problems are everywhere and we cannot escape them; so it is in our best interest to learn problem solving skills.
2. The more you solve problems, the stronger that part of your brain becomes, so it becomes easier.
3. Critical thinking is sometimes called "using your judgement", "thinking outside of the box" or even "thinking on your feet". It is an important skill that employers value.
4. It's okay to pause before you make certain decisions that have big implications for your life, safety and future.

5. A lot of information to help us with problems might be found using technology. However, we must be careful so that we are using technology ethically and not breaking any rules.

Chapter 5

HAVING A MENTOR

O nce upon a time, in a little town nestled between rolling hills, lived an 18-year-old young lady named Emily. She was a bright and ambitious young woman, eager to explore the 

world beyond her small community. Her parents were loving and wonderful but did not have a lot of academic training or experience outside of their town, so they often could not answer Emily's questions about university and the wider world. Despite her dreams, Emily often felt uncertain about her future. She craved guidance and inspiration to navigate the complexities of adulthood.

One afternoon, fate intervened when Emily attended a local community event. There, she met a warm and seasoned professional named Mr. Anderson, who had achieved remarkable success in his field. Intrigued by his knowledge and humble demeanor, Emily mustered the courage to approach him.

As they struck up a conversation, Mr. Anderson recognized the spark of potential in Emily's eyes. He saw a reflection of his younger self, full of aspirations and hunger for knowledge. Without hesitation, he offered to mentor Emily, believing that he could be the guiding light she needed.

Over the next few months, the bond between Emily and Mr. Anderson grew stronger. They met regularly, and during their sessions, Mr. Anderson shared valuable life experiences, insights, and practical advice. He listened to Emily's dreams and fears, helping her untangle the web of uncertainties that had clouded her mind. He met her parents, and they offered him fruit and vegetables from their garden as a means of paying him for his time, but he declined. He happily accepted the warm bowl of soup and homemade lemonade they offered, though.

Under Mr. Anderson's mentorship, Emily's confidence blossomed. She took on new challenges with enthusiasm, knowing she had a wise and caring advisor by her side. His encouragement fueled her determination to pursue her passions, and she set her sights on attending college to study environmental science, a field that had always captured her heart.

Beyond academic guidance, Mr. Anderson taught Emily essential life skills—time management, effective communication, and the power of perseverance. Their mentorship went beyond the boundaries of professional development, becoming a profound friendship based on mutual respect and admiration.

As time passed, Emily's hard work and dedication bore fruit. She secured a scholarship to her dream college and graduated with honors. Throughout her journey, Mr. Anderson remained a steadfast presence, cheering her on from the sidelines.

Years later, as a successful environmental scientist, Emily looked back on her path with immense gratitude. She knew that without Mr. Anderson's guidance, she might have faltered. His unwavering belief in her potential had ignited a fire within, propelling her forward even in moments of doubt.

Their story became a symbol of the profound impact mentorship can have on shaping young lives. Emily vowed to pay it forward by becoming a mentor herself, just like the guiding light that Mr. Anderson had been for her.

In this journey of life, the period of leaving teenage years and entering adulthood is often a time of uncertainty. It's a time when youthful dreams, aspirations, and uncertainties collide. Navigating this crucial phase can be overwhelming, but thankfully, no one has to go it alone. The power of guidance and support cannot be underestimated during these transformative years.

--- Enter mentorship ---the invaluable bond between an experienced individual and a young person seeking guidance. Mentorship is like having a trusted guide by your side, a wise companion who can illuminate the path ahead, provide advice, and instill confidence. It's a relationship built on mutual trust, respect, and a shared belief in the potential of the mentee.

Why is it important to have a mentor?

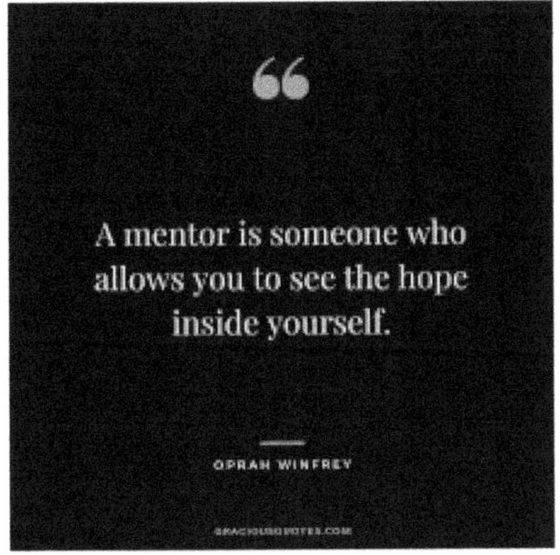

<u>Here is a secret many don't know</u>!!! If you want to make sure you make the right choices to achieve your professional and personal goals quickly and you want to avoid certain mistakes and learn from someone who has reached where you want to go, find a mentor.

It is best to find someone who is in the field that you aspire to be in and who has accomplished enough that he or she can pull you up as much as possible.

A mentor is a guide, an advisor and a role model.

Some of the key qualities of an effective mentor are:

1. Experience
2. Knowledge

3.   A willingness to work with a young person

Benefits of mentoring

Some of the benefits of mentoring are the following:

- Having access to an older role model – You have a front row seat to how the person operates and are able to ask questions and follow what practices appeal to you.
- Learning new things you won't necessarily learn in school – With all the time at school used for basic maths, geography, etc., many things about business, work and other parts of life were not taught.
- Being pulled out of your comfort zone – It is a wonderful thing when someone can see your potential and when you feel timid or not ready, draw you out so that instead of hiding in your insecurity, you are stretched to explore possibilities.
- Developing more self-confidence – When someone pours a lot into you, you learn more, know more, are capable of more and this can build your self-confidence and your self-esteem.
- Expanding your social skills and networking opportunities – If you are lucky, your mentor may

occasionally take you to events or introduce you to other influential persons, building your network. Observing others will also help you to learn how to behave in professional social settings.

- ◆ Being challenged– A mentor will challenge you when your thought patterns are faulty or when your behaviour is not consistent with success. This is essential for growth.
- ◆ Exploring career options – A mentor can act in the role of a coach and by asking the right questions and observing your natural inclinations help you to look at avenues for possible career paths that suit who you are and fits your goals.

Actually, the mentor can also benefit from the relationship; he or she can derive some personal satisfaction from the knowledge that he or she is helping someone, that person can develop further leadership skills and be recognized in the business community as one who is a positive influence.

When you are approaching someone to be your mentor, that person who has achieved a certain position in life will want to make sure he or she is not wasting time. So you might have to convince this person that you are serious and will take the relationship seriously.

Hello Mrs. Peters:

I hope you're doing well. I've been thinking a lot about my personal and professional growth and I've come to realize that your expertise and guidance would be incredibly valuable to me. I admire your achievements and from what I know of you, you seem to have accomplished some of the things I would like to accomplish myself.

I genuinely believe that having a mentor like you would help me gain new perspectives, refine my skills, and navigate the next steps in my journey. Your experience aligns perfectly with my aspirations, and I'd be honoured if you'd consider being my mentor.

Note that someone might decline your request because of being busy or already having too many mentees. Don't take it personally. You can thank the person for responding and ask him or her to recommend someone or just move on to the #2 person on your list.

You will have to make it clear to the person what you need. Take a moment to reflect on what would help you to move forward in your life. What are your personal and professional goals? In what areas are you lacking? What are your personal value systems, where do you most need guidance?

Mentors can be found in professional organizations, through personal connections, on college campuses, at your local Chamber of Commerce, etc.

Here are some considerations for you as a young person to find the best mentor for you:

- ◆ Clarifying your goals. It is important that you have a clear idea of what you want or where you want to go. This will help you to decide who is the best person to guide you on your journey. Some mentors are better with personal development, some with academic pursuits, and others with career development.
- ◆ Look for compatibility in values. A mentor relationship thrives on mutual respect and having something in common. Compatibility makes for a more meaningful connection.
- ◆ Experience and Expertise. Not only do you want someone who has been doing good things for a long enough time, but also someone who is good at what he or she does. If you are interested in engineering, then someone with a solid

background in mentoring can provide valuable insights and industry knowledge.

♦ Accessibility and ability to commit. Even if someone is experienced to the max and extremely knowledgeable, if that person is never available, constantly busy and does not return your calls or emails, then that person might not be the best fit as your mentor. The person must be willing to invest time and effort into the mentoring relationship.

♦ Approachable. You do not want to choose someone whom you find intimidating. As a mentee, you are likely to have a lot of questions, maybe even experience doubt, and the whole point of the experience is to be able to have meaningful interaction so choose someone with whom you feel comfortable.

♦ Networking Opportunities. It is always good to ensure the person you approach to mentor you has the potential to help you expand your network. You want someone who is well-connected in his or her field or is a member of a business network – someone who can help you get internships or introduce you to people who can, depending on the nature of the mentorship required.

- ◆ Positive Role model. A mentor can also be a role model who inspires you to be your best self. Therefore, if the person is constantly engaging in questionable behaviour or does not seem to have integrity, then maybe that person is not the best mentor for you.

After you have figured out precisely what you need, who you want to approach and made your request… the person might not be available. Hence, it's always good to have a Plan B and C and 2 other persons as backups.

At the first meeting, it is good to lay the foundation for the relationship – how often you will meet, expectations on both ends and what you as a mentee can bring to the table.

Challenges may arise when there is time conflict, when your mentor and you disagree or if there is a fundamental change in values. If this happens, just pause, and see if the relationship can be saved. Disagreement in and of itself is not bad, especially when it leads to learning and a new way of doing things.

Also, remember to keep the relationship professional and not get personally involved. That is not the reason for this relationship.

All in all, mentorship is a positive thing. You get to learn from a successful person and there is a great opportunity for you to grow and develop a level of self-confidence. In time, you might be in a position to mentor others.

Extra Credit: 5 things to Remember

1. Always choose someone who has reached or passed a place where you want to be yourself.
2. You can offer to be of value to your mentoring by volunteering an hour of your time per week to help that person or sharing a skill you have.
3. An in-person mentor is way better than following a celebrity on social media that you hardly know.
4. Your mentor will not always tell you what you want to hear, but looking at another perspective is a good thing.
5. Choose someone with integrity as your mentor

Chapter 6

HOW TO GET ALONG WITH PEOPLE?

Unless you plan to leave planet Earth because you are wealthy enough to purchase a planet for yourself, you are stuck here and will have to deal with all kinds of people.  Some of them are nice, but many of them are far from being qualified as nice people. At home, at school, at work, on public transportation, in the supermarket; even virtually, we both know that just because people are not physically in your space, doesn't mean they cannot irritate the life out of you.

So therefore, to prevent being arrested for getting physical with someone who irritated or angered you, or even to prevent your parents from being called to say you are being disrespectful, and especially for the sake of peace and to exist in harmony with other humans, let's spend some time looking at how to get along with people.

Why?

One of the first things you may ask yourself is, why is it important to get along with others? Or why should you even care? Well, because we can't be isolated all the time. Even if by nature, you are not an outgoing person and you stay alone as much as possible, you still have to communicate and interact with others – family members, other students for group projects, people you work with, etc. Life is better when you can have a harmonious relationship with others; you have less stress, fewer arguments, and you have one less thing to worry about. It's a win-win situation; learning people skills can greatly improve your life.

Self-control will grow muscles when you decide that getting along with others is something that you want to do. Being in control of yourself is a skill you will get better at as you choose who you want your companions and friends to be. These choices will play an important role in your experiences, and the individuals who you choose to get along with can sometimes become special persons in your life.

One of the biggest lessons we learned during the COVID-19 pandemic was that it would be a world of misery if we did not have others who could be around and communicate with us. It also showed us the importance of getting along with those whom we share a home with, so that instead of feeling trapped and irritated by those we have to be around, we could instead be happy for the time to build stronger bonds and spend quality time with those that you love.

When it comes to getting along with others in this wonderful world filled with so many different individuals, it would be helpful if you practice the following rules and apply them to your lives:

Pay attention to different types of personalities

Clearly, everyone is not the same. You might have had some teachers whose voices and manners made you want to crawl under your desk. Then there are some whose company you could have stayed in for hours after class was finished. People can be difficult in different ways and at varying intensities. Here are some types you might have encountered that you might want to minimize your contact with to avoid problems.

- The "gossiper" who talks about everyone and spreads information – truthful or not; this person always wants to be the one to share juicy details of someone's life, and often negative information. Spending too much time with this person might cause him or her to talk about you also, based on what you say to the person, or even what you didn't say. Be careful and don't share any private information with gossipers.

- Those who like to control. This is someone who might exert peer pressure on you; you feel as if you must follow him or her to be accepted or liked as a friend. Stay away from people who try to control you because you have your own personality, with your own taste, your likes and dislikes and it's always best for you to do what's right, rather than what someone wants you to do; this can include things like smoking or having sex when you are not even ready for these steps. Don't be manipulated.

- Persons who defy authority. Stay away from other young persons who insist on breaking rules or being rude and disrespectful to those in authority.

It's okay to speak up for yourself, but don't just be defiant for the sake of it... we don't have to agree with certain behaviours of our parents, the police, our school or college principals, etc., but let's give adults the respect they are due. Life will be a lot easier.

♦ Aggressive and brawling persons. Have you noticed the increase in fights and conflicts in schools and also the violence in our communities? You don't want to be involved in that kind of behaviour... neither as a perpetrator nor as a victim. Therefore, try not to hang around with persons who pick fights, who carry around weapons, or who are always exhibiting violence or anger-management issues.

" The most important single ingredient in the formula of success is knowing how to get along with people."

-

Theodre Roosevelt

Avoiding persons who fit the descriptions above and some others that you can think of who you know are toxic, will help you to lead a lot more pleasant and peaceful life.

So let's get to it... how do you get along fabulously with others? There is a book called, "How to Win Friends and Influence People" written by Dale Carnegie. Although the book was written a while back, the good points are still relevant today. Here are five tips that stand out from his book.

1. Something as simple as smiling can make a big difference in how you are perceived by others.
2. Give people your full attention when they are speaking and listen without interruption.
3. Ask questions.
4. Show genuine interest in others.
5. Let people know what you appreciate about them.
6. Listen and try to avoid arguments.
7. If possible, I would suggest you read the whole book, when you can.

 # Don't react to everything 

Sometimes, you will find yourself in an uncomfortable situation. It is very important that you observe what is happening and try to figure out what is causing the problem and make a decision if to stay in that space or to walk away. Do not react to everything happening around you. If someone is shouting, you don't have to shout back... someone who is pushing for a confrontation or a fight, unless that person hits you, make sure you stay as calm as possible. Calmness is a superpower. You will be provoked in this life...but don't react. You will be lied on, disrespected and maybe even the subject of rumours, but to react like the person doing you wrong will make you just like they are. Choose to be better.

I'm not saying it is easy, but I'm saying it is worth it. *Try to be the cool-headed one.*

Nature has given us the impulse to react immediately to problems, usually by running away or fighting. During confrontations at work, the impulse of combat usually prevails. Our reflex to flee or fight is a way to protect ourselves from being eaten by other aggressive species. Even though these habits date back millennia, we are still programmed to respond to aggression by experiencing the same physiological changes, such as a stomach ache, increased heart rate and so on, which tell us that we need to "confront the enemy"!

Pick your battles

Choose your battles because you cannot win them all. Sometimes you have to let the little things go so you can focus your energy on the issues that are really important to you. Remember the guy who cried wolf? If you make a whole story out of the smallest things you encounter, no one will listen to you when it comes to dealing with a really important problem. You may be surprised that your approach to a 'so-called battle' can be the difference in the way the situation ends. Frustration from another person being expressed in a negative way can have positive results if ignored or you choose to handle it with a less aggressive response.

Practice Empathy

Sometimes it helps to put yourself in others' shoes and try to understand their situation. People behave differently based on their situations, and although we might find them annoying at first, when we understand that they are that way because of a particular situation, we can understand them better.

Don't take everything personally

If a classmate is always shouting, you might find it annoying. If your neighbour always cuts his yard on Sunday mornings with a loud lawnmower, you might find it inconvenient and irritating. But I can bet you all the money in your pocket, that they are doing whatever they are doing because it's convenient or a habit. They are not setting out to get to you. So stop taking people's behaviours personally, and you will likely get along with them much better.

Conclusion

Difficult people do not just create minefields, they are minefields. Their disruptive behaviour slows productivity, compromises deadlines and influences the commitment of their colleagues' life and work. You need to find strategies that will help you deal with this type of individual. Not only will it show your ability to solve problems, but it will also set the tone for appropriate and supportive behaviour within your department. Your true team spirit and the importance you place on success will be noted.

Keep this in mind; you won't get along with everyone, but as long as you are sincere and you show a genuine interest in others, you might find some things that may be similar to yourself and you will be able to get along with any individual that you may encounter, whether it be for a couple of minutes, several hours or for long durations throughout your day and life. Differences between individuals are not always bad, when you try to understand people; it is a key method of fixing conflicts quickly and building healthy and lasting relationships.

Parents should teach teens that healthy relationships occur when both people:

- ◆ Care about each other.
- ◆ Understand and respect each other and are responsible for each other.
- ◆ Solve problems together and communicate with honesty.
- ◆ Share at least some of the same goals and values.

Extra Credit: 5 things to remember

1. We have to share space with so many other people so it makes sense to try to live as peacefully as possible. To do so takes time and effort, practicing patience, empathy, good communication skills and more patience.

2. Choose to be around the type of person who will add value to your life experiences by making the right choices and having good behaviours towards others and themselves.

3. Respect people's right to be different. Some will think differently from you, and that's okay. Just as you want to be respected for who you are, others want that too.

4. Decide what you would like to react to. Every situation has a different level of reaction, your time and energy are very important. So, you should use them like very rare gold coins.

5. Showing people that they are important by taking the time to listen, asking them different questions, showing interest and also letting them know that you appreciate them are great ways to influence others positively.

Chapter 7

FINANCIAL LITERACY: MONEY 101

Alright, future millionaires, gather around! We're diving into the magical world of money, and trust me, it's not as intimidating as you think. So, grab your snacks and let's embark on this epic quest into the land of budgeting, saving, investing, and credit – the keys to financial awesomeness.

Once Upon a Broke Time

Meet Sarah, your typical 17-year-old girl with a passion for sneakers and a knack for spending her allowance faster than a pizza delivery. One day, after finding herself staring at an empty wallet, with her parents refusing to give her more allowance, Sarah decided it was time to level up and learn the secrets of financial literacy. She was tired of seeing her neighbours live lavishly while her parents always had to scrimp and save and do without the basics. She decided this was not going to be her life forever.

Sarah consulted a much older uncle who was well off and he taught her the basics as we will see in this chapter. She started making some small changes; she tracked her spending for a month and realized she was dropping more money at the smoothie shop than she thought. So, she created a budget, a master plan for her allowance.

Budgeting - The Hero of Every Paycheck

Budgeting is like choosing your character in a video game – it determines the path of your financial journey. Picture this: you've got a stash of gold coins (your monthly allowance), and you need to decide how to use them wisely.

In the world of budgeting, your primary weapons are your income and expenses. Income is the loot you earn, whether it's from your part-time job, allowance, or any side hustle you've got going on. Expenses are the dragons you'll face – those sneaky creatures that try to gobble up your cash.

Sit down with a pen and paper or your smartphone, and list your sources of income (you have a chapter on How to make money so you have no excuses to not have any). Track your spending for a month and categorize your expenses into different areas like snacks, entertainment, top-up, etc.

You can consider essentials – things you can't do without like food, transport if you have to take the bus and for many of you, phone-related expenses. Then you have non-essentials like movies, in-game purchases, and other fun stuff.

Please consider putting aside something for future goals like college or a vehicle of your own. Many adults have an emergency fund, but ti's up to you if you want to consider that at this stage.

The division some people use is the 50-30-20 rule where 50% of your income is for essentials, 30% for non-essentials, and 20% for goals and emergency fund.

Pause right now and create a budget... then come back and continue reading.

Congratulations! You've crafted your budget but there's more! Regularly check your spending against your plan to see which areas need adjustment.

Be flexible, adapt, and know that it's likely that as you grow, so will your income, expenses, and financial goals.

Saving – Putting up something for the future

Now that Sarah has her budget game on point, it's time for the next level – saving. Saving isn't just for those making a lot of money; it's for you, too! Imagine saving up for a gift for your boyfriend or girlfriend, the latest gaming console, or even college.

Most banks offer savings accounts specifically designed for young people. Look for accounts with no or low fees and decent interest rates. This interest is what will make your money multiple over time. Seek out the best deals, because every cent counts.

The golden rule of saving is to pay yourself first so treat your savings as your first and most important expense. For some of you, tithing is important so please keep that in consideration so you give a tenth of your income to your offering.

Let's say your monthly allowance is 100 dollars. Before you allocate any of it to other categories (like essentials or non-essentials), set aside a predetermined amount for your savings account. This might be 10%, 20%, or whatever percentage aligns with your goals.

Saving without a goal is like embarking on a trip without a map – you might get somewhere, but you won't know if it's where you wanted to go. Define your financial quests. Is it a new gaming console, a trip with friends, or college fees.

Having clear goals will not only motivate you to save but also help you determine how much money you need to stash away and by when. Write down your goals and keep them in a visible place, like on your wall. This way, every time you add something to your savings, you'll know you're one step closer to achieving something great.

Adults often need an emergency fund in case they lose their jobs. This might not apply to you, but many young people like the option of having some money put away in case something wild happens...you can even sometimes lend your parents from this money, but be sure to negotiate a nice interest.

The key is to make saving a consistent part of your financial routine. As you grow, so should your treasure chest. By mastering the art of saving, you're building the foundation for a prosperous future.

Some creative ways of saving are:

1. Jar – keep a jar or piggy bank in the house and you put your change into it at the end of every week and keep only paper money.

2. Box hand – have a program with friends or family where you put aside maybe $10 or whatever you can afford each week and you get it at the end of every 6 months or so. Everyone takes turns taking a hand.

3. Savings Apps – Some apps take your change after a transaction and saves it for you and you redeem it at a specific time.

4. Have no spend weekends – designate certain weekends in the month where you will just engage in activities that require no cash.

5. Ask your parents what jobs they are willing to pay you for and keep a record of what you earn from them and decide with them when is the payout period. You can even ask them to match what you save.

6. If you have a job, you can ask your employer to take out a specific amount weekly or monthly for savings.

Investing – Planting a tree that will bear fruit

Investing sounds fancy, right? Especially for a young person with limited finances, but hey... it's not only about what you have, but about having important knowledge for when you do get more.

Investing is like planting seeds. You give up a few dollars to day to grow a forest of riches in the future. Instead of letting your money sit idly, you put it to work, and through the power of compound interest, watch it multiply over time.

There are various ways to embark on the investing quest. Stocks, bonds, mutual funds – think of them as different potions with unique effects. Stocks give you a share of ownership in a company, bonds are like loans to corporations or governments, and mutual funds pool your money with other persons invest in a diversified portfolio - that's the equivalent of not putting all your eggs in one basket.

Investing involves risk – after all, the greater the potential reward, the higher the risk. It's like choosing a game level – easy quests might have fewer rewards, while challenging ones offer greater treasures. Stocks, for instance, can be volatile, like a pitbull's temperament. They have the potential for high returns, but their value can also fluctuate. Bonds, on the other hand, are more stable but offer lower returns. Diversifying your investments, spreading your money across different potions, helps manage risk.

The true power of investing lies in the magic of compound interest. The earlier you start investing, the more time your gold has to grow. Let's say you invest 100 gold coins today. With a reasonable rate of return, it might double in a decade. Fast forward another decade, and it could quadruple. Time is your greatest friend in this regards

By the way, you can invest in someone else's business. If you have a friend who needs $1,000 to start buying and selling phones, you can offer $200 from your savings with an agreement that you receive back 200 a month for 10 months, which lands you with $2,000 in 10 months – much more interest than the bank. Be sure you trust someone before you put your money with them though and that they know what they are doing.

Investing is the gateway to building long-term wealth. It's not about becoming an overnight millionaire; it's about setting up a financial fortress that stands the test of time. Arm yourself with knowledge, get sound advice, act wisely and many your investments be as prosperous as possible

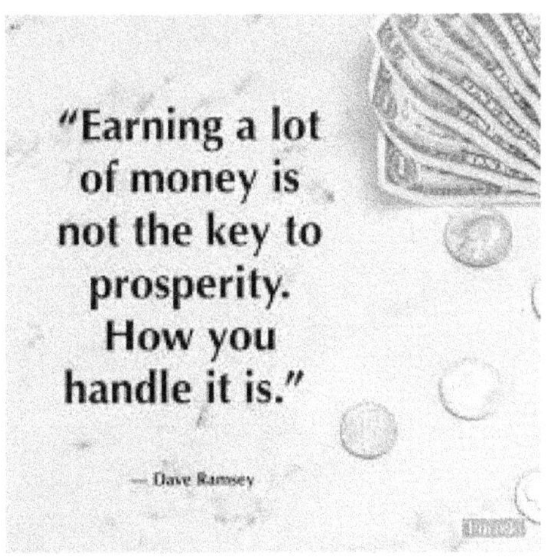

Credit - The Power-Up You Didn't Know You Needed

Credit is like a superpower. It can either make you fly or crash and burn. Our friend Sarah, in talking to her uncle, discovered that credit isn't just for adults in suits; even teenagers can start building it. Credit isn't just a plastic card; it's your key to navigating the vast financial landscape. It helps you to buy things or start your own business without having the cash right now. Credit is basically the trust that lenders like banks or credit card companies place in you to repay borrowed money.

When you use credit responsibly, you build a credit history. Think of it as your financial resume, showcasing your ability to manage money wisely. A good credit history opens doors to lower interest rates, better loan terms, and other financial opportunities.

Credit can be good or bad. Some people get carried away with spending money they don't have using credit cards and have difficulty paying back. The recommendation is to pay off credit card bills at the end of the month so they don't pile up as credit card interest rates are very very high. Here are a few tips on using credit wisely:

- ◆ Start small: Consider a secured credit card (you have enough money to cover the card) or become an authorized user on your parent's card to dip your toes into the credit waters.
- ◆ Pay On Time: Timely payments are the superhero moves in credit-building. Set up reminders so that you remember to pay on time to avoid late fees.
- ◆ Keep Balances Low: Don't max out your credit cards. Aim to use only a small portion of your available credit.

- Try not to buy too much on impulse or to engage in emotional spending where you shop whenever you feel down or angry.

Please also note that credit in the form of loans can be useful if you want a mortgage for your home or a car.

Needs Vs. Wants

It is always important to make a separation between needs and wants. If your parents have cooked dinner and there is food in the house, a pizza is a want. Being able to top-up your phone to use it could be a need. While nothing is wrong with eating out, we have to be sure all our money does not go into wants and into things that don't last. Sometimes the friends you hang out with have bad money habits or have no money and all of yours goes into feeding or paying movie tickets for everyone else. Generosity is good but if your goal is to save $100 a month, then you might have to decide if buying tickets for everyone is a need at this time.

While this chapter just touches the basics, there is so much more for you to learn about money. Check other books, talk to a parent or family member or check out good sources online.

Extra Credit: 5 Things to Remember

1. Do not let your age keep you from becoming a financial genius. The earlier you learn the better and the more you learn the better.

2. Don't get caught up with advertising that makes you spend all the time. Kepp a little something back so you always have a stash.

3. Have a budget so you know where your money goes and don't be afraid to ask for jobs from neighbours or community shops to earn extra cash.

4. Using credit is good because it helps to build your credit score which makes it easier to get more money when necessary.

5. Land is always a good thing to start investing in early because it appreciates (increases in value), while things like cars depreciate (lose value)

Chapter 8

How to Make Money?

It's always amusing when older people assume that because you are not paying rent or bills you don't need a lot of money. Well, you do need money because having your own money, means you don't

have to bother the older folks who do have rent and bills to pay. As a young person, you need money for your extra snacks, a pair of cool sneakers that you have permission to buy, hair products, phone top-up, movies, transportation, and extra clothes above and beyond what is provided and whatever else suits you...maybe money for games or personal hygiene items you don't' want to ask for.

The long and short of it is that YOU NEED CASH! In a way that is legal and parent-approved.

Allowances? Yes, they come sometimes. That is if your parents can afford to give it. If they can't, don't let it get to you. After all, they have to keep a roof over your head, pay electricity and water bills, buy food, school supplies, pay insurance and a bunch of other stuff that comes with being an adult. If however, they offer an allowance, be sure to show your appreciation for it. As you get older, you can negotiate for more, but make sure you know that they can afford it. Negotiation is not just putting on a cute face and puppy dog eyes... it is a strategic way of approaching a situation where both persons can come out winners. We will discuss this is detail in another chapter.

So....are you young and looking for new ways to earn money? Well, you are in the right place and reading the right things at the right time!

Are you allowed to work under 18?

Yes, while it is true that in some places, child labour is illegal, in most places, children are allowed to do little job to make some pocket change. I'm sure you have heard of or seen teenagers packing grocery bags, having lemonade stands, delivering newspapers (back in the day) and wrapping presents at Christmas.

The Internet offers a wide range of opportunities, websites and applications that allow us to earn money in exchange for doing work online and it is also a good way to promote your services to third parties.

Although it is true that you can start looking for income outside the Internet, you, as a teenager, have an advantage over older people and that is that you have grown up with the technology so you understand it well. You are probably an expert in social media, you know how to use apps and you have the ability to create videos and those skills are the ones to take advantage of. Look at TikTok and you will see a lot of young persons making videos with so many followers and shares.

First Things First

Here are the first things to consider before you jump into the working world:

- Get your parents' permission. For this to work well, it is important that you discuss with mom, dad or both the following –
- What you plan to do to make this extra money

- ◆ Where you plan to work
- ◆ How many hours you can work without it affecting your school work and household chores
- ◆ What you use the money for
- ◆ Figure out what you need money for. Be clear on what you are working for... tuition money, money for clothes, to help at home, etc.? Some can be used for immediate and short term needs like transportation or school supplies, some for the medium term like saving for tuition for the next term and you can consider long-range goals like college or a trip overseas.
- ◆ What kind of work you will do. This will depend on a few things:
- ◆ What do you like? If you like being on the computer, then a computer related job might seem easier for you, because you will be on it anyway, so why not profit from it?
- ◆ What are you good at? Doing something that you really suck at might make it hard for you and will not make the work pleasant or you might not even be seen as having the ability to do that particular work. Raise your hands if you have seen someone singing for a competition and you think, "he just can't even sing"?

- ◆ What can actually make money? Even if you like bathing pets, if no one is interested in paying for it, then it's not profitable.

Legitimate ways to earn money as a young person

Let's now get to the meat of the matter.... Ways to make money! Go through this list and see which ones can work for you.

Run errands

Many persons need their utility bills paid, groceries picked up or other errands done but don't have the time or the ability. You can do these errands for them. Even if you have started college, chances are you will have some time flexibility.

Get a job as a packer in a supermarket

Larger supermarkets often need persons to pack the groceries on the shelves, or pack the bags at the cashier counter and even take the bags to the customer's car.

Painting

If you see someone in your neighbourhood doing construction, you can ask about helping with painting. It's easy to learn. Maybe you can ask to do something simple like the fence if you don't want to take the chance on something as big as part of the house.

Yard work

You can use your parents' weedwhacker or lawn mower and cut other people's yards. Using your equipment might also mean having a rake handy. Some persons will have their own yard tools, so you can just get the job and show up and do the work. Remember to do it well and don't cut corners. Once you do it well, they are likely to call you to come back and also refer you to their friends.

Baby sitting

If you got paid for all the times you watched your baby brother or sister in your own home, you would probably have some good change in your wallet right now...LOL. Well, the skills you picked up... patience, learning to make hot dogs, knowing which channels had nice child-friendly shows, saying "NO" 20 times in an hour and handing them back over to your parents in one piece and the house still standing is a skill you can get paid for in other families.

Photography

Many newspapers and online users pay for high-quality unique photographs. If you have an excellent phone camera or digital camera and you have an eye for beauty and light and shadows, etc., then you can sell your photos.

Video creation and editing

Some teenagers are boss at putting together videos using still pictures and sound; are you one of them? You can do ads for entrepreneurs who don't have those skills. There are many free software and apps online that can help you to put together a professional-looking video.

Graphic Design & Flyer Creation

For those of you who are proficient at using Canva or Microsoft Publisher, you could design logos, flyers or brochures for persons to advertise their business or to publicize an event.

Social Media Poster

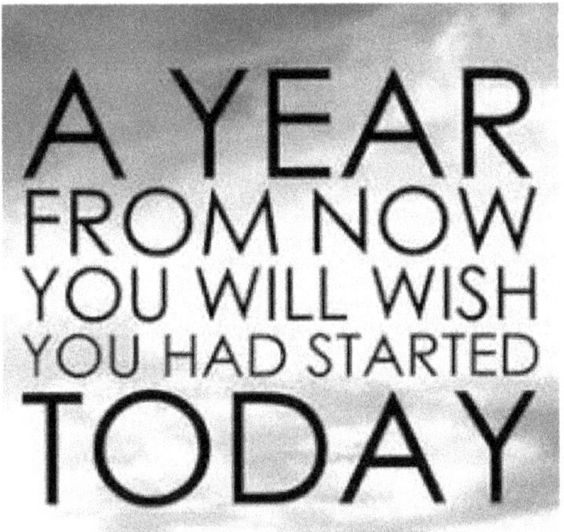

Stop laughing... I don't mean for you to be a physical poster on someone's wall... I mean to post on someone social media's account for them?. The person gives you the content and their Facebook or Instagram password and you make the posts, once or twice weekly as he or she wants them. This saves them time and you get to make money; a win-win for both of you.

Tutoring

After all the time you spent in school, I'm sure you mastered certain subjects. Studies have shown that people learn easier from their peers; that means, having graduated from secondary school, you can now help other persons who are in 5th Form (12th grade in some countries). You can even help students who are in Primary School.

House cleaning

Around Christmas, many persons are happy to get help to clean windows and do other chores at their home. Some even bring in teenagers to help to prepare for home parties or dinners or other events.

Dog walker

If you are a lover of animals and your neighbour has dogs that are not vicious, then you can offer to take them walking for exercise. This way the dogs get a chance to run and play and your neighbour gets to have 20 extra minutes for his or her chores.

Restaurant Work

Places that sell food often need persons to serve, wash dishes or help with tidying up. Of course, you have to be careful not to break anything or you might have to pay for it, but you should be able to get a reasonable sum of money.

Take online surveys

There are many websites that pay users to take surveys and give their opinions on different things. For some, you have to be at least 18 years or older, and for others, you can participate even if you are younger. Be careful about scammers and don't give out personal details online unless you verify that it is a legitimate website.

Sell things you don't use

Look for items in very good condition, take a nice photograph of them and post on Facebook, Instagram or Ebay. Craigslist is also an option in some locations. You can sell clothing, electronics or any other game or item you don't need and others do need.

Sell items for others

Some of your relatives and friends might have things they want to sell but they are not necessarily online. You can offer to post the items for them and get a commission from the sale. You can also pay them a small fee for the item and sell it for more to make a profit.

Get paid for your skills

What might seem easy and basic to you may seem like a lot for someone else. You can sign up with sites like Fiverr, Freelancer or Upwork and provide services for others who need it. You can offer skills such as writing, editing, translating, animation for streamers or even creating trailers for video games.

Create a simple website

You can use WordPress and create websites for small business owners. Once you do one, get a recommendation or reference to share with prospective customers. Offer your services to individual or businesses telling them of your interest to build their site for a fee Create a good cover letter and say what you know how to do. Today many jobs can be done without leaving home and this is an advantage.

Teach seniors

How many times have you been asked by your parents, aunts, uncles or older persons at your church to help them with something online? Surely, more than once! Then take advantage of this to earn some extra income. You can even hold a class for 3 or 4 persons at a time to teach them. This method will require a lot of patience but it is certainly doable!

Create a Youtube channel

YouTube is a fantastic place to share valuable information that will educate or entertain people. Once you upload videos on a regular basis and get many visitors and subscribers to your site, you can then monetize your site by allowing ads on your site.

Extra Credit: 5 things to Remember

1. Money is good but you should always be mindful of what you are using it for.
2. Working at a young age teaches you responsibility, habits of diligence, putting out good effort and budgeting
3. If you are under 18, be mindful of the laws and policies for working in your area.
4. Learn as much as you can while working; that knowledge will come in handy.
5. Remember to save some of what you earn

Chapter 9

STRESS MANAGEMENT & SELF CARE

Emma, a 17-year-old student, found herself overwhelmed and stressed out. She was juggling schoolwork, extracurricular activities, and personal relationships. Recently, she has been feeling exhausted, anxious, and struggling to focus on her tasks. Recognizing the need to prioritize her well-being, Emma embarked on a journey to practice self-care.

One evening, Emma sat down in her room, surrounded by piles of textbooks, assignments, and unfinished projects with a killer headache.

She took a deep breath and decided it was time to make a change. She began by acknowledging her feelings and reminding herself that her well-being was just as important as her academic success.

Emma started by creating a schedule to manage her time effectively. She put down school time and homework time and knowing how much better she felt when she was active, she included some time for exercise. She decided to do short walks with her dog and then downloaded a Zumba app to do some of that twice a week as she loved the music.

Emma reached out to her two closest friends, telling them how overwhelmed she felt. They offered to do the Zumba classes with her and to take time out to have a group chat weekly to talk about how they were feeling. Emma realized that talking about her feelings helped alleviate her stress. Initially, she wasn't sure if they would think she was just being a drama queen, but she was happy they understood and they themselves felt like they needed to slow down. She started scheduling regular hangouts with them, creating a space to relax and have fun outside of her academic responsibilities.

One of her friends suggested they also try colouring books and painting and they found some cheap books and supplies to use. This creative process she noticed helped her to forget stress, parents arguing, and school work deadlines.

It wasn't easy for Emma to give herself so much time because she was raised to be a high-achiever and felt she had to constantly push herself so she didn't get left behind, especially knowing her parents had high expectations for her. However, when one of her friends blurted out, "girl, you need to give yourself a break and chill", she laughingly was reminded that it was okay to take breaks, make mistakes, and ask for help when needed.

As Emma continued her self-care journey, she began to notice positive changes. Her stress levels decreased, she had fewer headaches, and she actually felt more focused and motivated in her studies. She made up her mind to have a better balance between school work and her personal life, making sure she dedicated time for relaxation and self-reflection.

Through her journey of stress management and self-care, Emma realized that she deserved to prioritize her well-being. She understood that by taking care of herself, she would be better able to navigate the challenges of her teenage years with a sense of inner peace.

Being a teenager can be an exciting time, but it also brings its fair share of challenges. Juggling schoolwork, social pressures, and personal growth can sometimes lead to stress, and impact your mental well-being. In this chapter, we will explore practical strategies for stress management, nurturing your mental health, and practicing self-care. By developing these skills, you can build resilience, maintain balance, and navigate the teenage years with a greater sense of well-being.

What exactly is stress?

Stress is a normal reaction to change. It can result in physical and emotional tension. Small amounts of stress might not be so bad, especially if it pushes us to study for a test we are worried about, or to avoid bad people. However, prolonged stress over a period of time can really affect us negatively.

Some of the things that cause stress for youth could be:

- A lot of school work or pressure to do well at school
- Expectations of parents and adults

- ♦ Being unhappy at home
- ♦ Their physical appearance
- ♦ Peer pressure
- ♦ Relationship matters

Also, there are often so many big decisions to make after leaving high school – college, work, rest, etc. Decisions cannot even be made only on what you want, but what parents want and can afford, and the family's need for money.

The Impact of Stress on Mental Health

Chronic stress over time leaves a person feeling overwhelmed and can often lead to anxiety and depression which seems to be more common in youth than people realize, but who feels it knows it. It is important that you take care of yourself. Avoid as much stress as you can and deal with things as they pop up.

The potential consequences of prolonged stress on your emotional well-being are as follows.

- ♦ Anxiety and Depression: Being stressed for a long time or having a lot of stress at once can cause you to feel anxious or depressed. You might find yourself having shortness of breath, feeling light-headed, dizzy, sweating and other symptoms of anxiety or having low interest in most things, low energy, not wanting to get out of bed, having appetite changes, feeling sad and so on. We don't want to get to this point.

♦ Cognitive Functioning: High levels of stress can affect your ability to get your school work done, your ability to focus and sometimes even to remember simple things. It becomes harder to think clearly, concentrate, solve problems, make decisions and retain information when under chronic stress.

♦ Sleep Disturbances: Stress can disrupt sleep patterns, leading to difficulties falling asleep, staying asleep, or experiencing restful sleep. Lack of sleep can further cause you to be even more stressed which can negatively affect your feelings of well-being.

♦ Physical Symptoms: Stress can affect you physically, causing headaches, muscle tension, stomach problems, and a weakened immune system which means you could catch colds and other illnesses pretty easily.

♦ Interpersonal Difficulties: Stress can affect your relationships with friends, family or others, as individuals under significant stress may become irritable, withdrawn, or have difficulty managing emotions. The resulting conflicts and strained social connections can further contribute to feelings of isolation and distress.

It is very important that persons deal with stress very early before it becomes too overbearing. Be proactive about stress management and do not allow it to get out of control.

Stress Management Techniques

Here are some things that you can do to help you manage your stress...Use whichever techniques work better for you:

Deep Breathing Exercises: Practice deep breathing exercises to help calm the mind and body. Take slow, deep breaths, inhaling through the nose and exhaling through the mouth. Focus on the sensation of the breath entering and leaving your body, allowing it to bring a sense of relaxation.

Mindfulness Meditation: Engage in mindfulness meditation to help you feel grounded in the moment and reduce stress. Find a quiet space, sit comfortably, and focus your attention on the sensations of your breath or the environment around you. When your mind wanders, gently bring your focus back to the present moment.

Physical Activity: Engage in regular physical activity to release built-up tension and boost your mood. Find activities you enjoy, such as dancing, jogging, playing a sport, or swimming. Exercise helps release endorphins, which can improve mood and reduce stress levels.

Time Management: Learn effective time management skills to reduce stress related to schoolwork and other responsibilities. Prioritize tasks, break them into smaller, manageable steps, and create a schedule or to-do list. Set realistic goals and allocate dedicated time for relaxation and self-care.

Healthy Sleep Habits: Establish a consistent sleep routine to ensure you get sufficient rest. Aim for 7-9 hours of sleep each night. Create a calming bedtime routine and try not to eat too close to sleeping time. I know this might be hard for you as a young person, but try to ease up on screen time before bed because it affects the quality of your sleep. Make sure your room is cool and your bed is clean and comfortable. Trust me, a good night's sleep can really does much to reduce stress and improve your mood.

Social Support: Seek support from trusted friends, family members, or mentors when you're feeling stressed. Share your concerns and emotions with someone who can offer guidance or simply provide a listening ear. Spending time with loved ones and engaging in positive social connections can help alleviate stress. In-person connections are important.

Creative Outlets: Engage in creative activities that help express emotions and provide a sense of relaxation. This can include drawing, painting, writing, playing a musical instrument, or engaging in crafts. Creativity allows for self-expression and serves as a healthy outlet for stress relief.

Journaling: Keep a journal to write down your thoughts, emotions, and experiences. Journaling can help you process and reflect on stressful situations, gain clarity, and promote self-awareness. It's a good tool for dumping thoughts from your head unto paper. Write freely without judgment, and explore different perspectives and solutions. Make sure you keep it somewhere where there is privacy.

Limit Technology and Screen Time: Take breaks from excessive screen time and limit exposure to social media or other online sites that may contribute to stress. Create boundaries and set time for activities that don't involve screens, such as reading, spending time in nature, or engaging in hobbies.

Seeking Help: If stress becomes overwhelming, or impacts your daily life significantly, don't hesitate to seek professional help. Reach out to a school counselor, therapist, or mental health professional who can provide guidance, support, and tools to manage stress effectively.

Remember, do what works for you as an individual. Try different strategies, give them time to work and as much as you can, develop good habits. Ensure you hang out with people who are calming and non-toxic.

Promote Self-Awareness & Self-Reflection

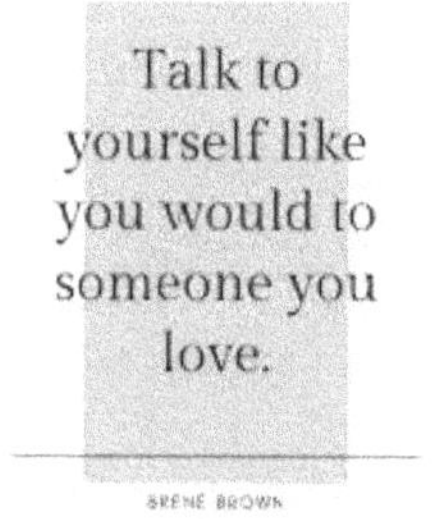

Self-awareness means understanding who you are – your thoughts, emotions, beliefs, your personality, what motivates you, and understanding how they all affect your behavior.

Self-reflection is about pausing to contemplate questions such as, who am I? Why do I feel the way I do? Why do I react the way I do? What makes me feel calm? Who or what makes me angry or why? Etc.

It is always important to recognize your feelings at any given time and validate them. If the feeling is a negative one, try to understand what triggered it and how you can deal with it for a positive outcome. We can't fight all our feelings but at least we can understand why we feel how we do.

Practice self-compassion and self-acceptance. Give yourself the love you need and be gentle with yourself. Stop beating yourself up for things you have no control over and just accept who you are. It's not your fault where you were born, who your parents are or how you look... just make the best of what you have and when you are able, you can change what you can.

Address the importance of breaking stigmas surrounding mental health and seeking support without shame or judgment

Self-Care Practices

Taking care of yourself physically, mentally, emotionally, socially and spiritually is important. Don't neglect your self-care because you are in school or overwhelmed. That's the very thing that will help you to cope with what's going on in your life. Here are some self-care tips:

80+ SELF CARE ACTIVITIES FOR TEENS

Kiddie Matters-Coaching Kids For Success

1. Listen to music
2. Take a shower
3. Talk to a friend
4. Watch a movie
5. Read a book
6. Go for a walk
7. Ride your bike
8. Exercise
9. Play with your pet
10. Stretch your muscles
11. Do yoga
12. Meditate or pray
13. Talk to a friend on the phone
14. Go the park with a friend*
15. Go to the mall*
16. Get a hair cut*
17. Take a nap
18. Plan an outing with friends*
19. Go for a jog
20. Write in a journal
21. Invite a friend to your house*
22. Go for a swim*
23. Go for a hike*
24. Try a new activity
25. Play board games
26. Play card games
27. Play a video game
28. Cook with your parent
29. Go to the spa with a parent
30. Go outside and watch the birds and other animals
31. Make a list of things you like about you
32. Go to the library
33. Write a poem/short story
34. Learn a new language
35. Sing your favorite songs
36. Write a song
37. Learn to play an instrument
38. Make a funny video
39. Draw or paint a picture
40. Make a list of your accomplishments
41. Make a bucket list
42. Write a letter to your future self
43. Make a list of things you're good at
44. Work outside in nature
45. Plant a garden*
46. Make a scrapbook
47. Trim your nails
48. Visit a museum*
49. Eat your favorite dessert
50. Take photos of nature
51. Make a playlist of your favorite songs
52. Do a puzzle
53. Play with a sibling
54. Go to the bookstore *
55. Google information about a different culture
56. Watch funny cat videos
57. Read a comic
58. Go outside and watch the clouds
59. Make a playlist of funny movies
60. Turn up the music and dance
61. Make a list of people you look up to and why
62. Practice deep breathing exercises
63. Walk barefoot in grass
64. Read an inspirational book
65. Write in a gratitude journal
66. Do an arts and craft activity
67. Start an art journal
68. Have a good laugh
69. Practice progressive muscle relaxation
70. Volunteer in your community*
71. Draw or color Zentangles
72. Draw or color Mandalas
73. Unplug and spend time in nature
74. Go stargazing
75. Make a fairy garden
76. Look at family photo albums
77. Read inspiring quotes
78. Listen to running water
79. Snuggle under a cozy blanket
80. Fly a kite
81. Write a love letter to yourself
82. Make jewelry
83. Blow bubbles and be silly
84. Give yourself a self-massage
85. Daydream

***Ask for your parent's permission**

©2018 Kiddie-matters.com

* Develop your personalized self-care routine*

On the journey of being a youth, prioritizing stress management, nurturing mental health, and practicing self-care are vital for overall well-being. By implementing the strategies discussed in this chapter, you can develop healthy coping mechanisms, practice self-care, and cultivate a greater sense of self-awareness. Remember, seeking help is a sign of strength, and taking care of your mental health is an ongoing process. Embrace self-care as a lifelong commitment, and navigate the teenage years with confidence, balance, and a thriving sense of well-being.

Extra Credit: 5 Things to remember

1. It is very, very important that no matter where you live, you recognize that there is no shame in asking for help. Whether it be a friend, counselor, pastor or even having to call a hotline, it's okay to reach out when you most need it.

2. Take at least 15 minutes daily to engage in some form of self-care... some activity or hobby that makes you feel happy, relaxed or balanced.

3. Taking a break from your screen is essential. Even social media sometimes can become depressing when we start comparing ourselves with others,

even knowing that some photos don't give the true picture of their lives.

4. Managing your time is key to managing stress. How do you spend the 24 hours you have been given? Do you pay attention to quality rest and make a list of priorities so important things get done first?

5. Love yourself with every ounce of your being. When you do, you will make your mental health a priority and you will be happier and healthier.

Chapter 10

THE ART OF NEGOTIATION

Parents set rules.

Teachers set rules

Employers set rules.

Private organizations set rules

Governments set rules

Churches set rules

Oftentimes, we can do our best to abide by the rules set out but sometimes, they don't seem to be too helpful to us. As a young person, just blatantly breaking rules is a sure path to disaster.

Ideally, the better route would be to have a discussion to negotiate for a different position than that which was set out by whomever it is in authority...parent, teacher or employer, etc.

The problem is if you have the kind of parent that will say, "I do not negotiate with terrorists"... LOL. Don't let that stop you; of course, you know it is meant as a joke. After all, you are young, almost innocent and seeking only the betterment of yourself and others. Right? Let's pretend that is the case.

Also, many people expect that as a youth, you will blindly accept what is placed before you. It would be good if everyone can see eye-to-eye and agree on everything, but it's unrealistic. Sometimes you will recognize that you want something different; maybe more or better than what is offered or expected and you are willing to speak up for it. To be able to manage these situations, it is in your best interest to learn and master *that skill, called NEGOTIATION*. With the art of negotiation, you have the power to make the most out of life by advocating for yourself, by sharing a different viewpoint, by creating a scenario where you are saying, "Can we discuss this because I would like something different from what you are offering?"

Now, what is the **ART OF NEGOTIATION?**

Before I explain this phrase, let me tell you a brief story about how powerful the power of negotiation can be.

Some time ago, in a small town, there lived an 18-year-old young man named David. He had a passionate dream of organizing a charity event to raise funds for underprivileged children's education. However, when approaching businesses, he was met with challenges and rejections.

Undeterred, David knew that the art of negotiation could be his ticket to success. He attended networking events, reaching out to potential sponsors through social media and email. Building personal connections, he genuinely showed interest in their businesses and values, forming meaningful partnerships.

Still, securing sponsorships proved difficult, as many cited budget constraints and prior commitments to other causes. Still Undeterred, David customized his proposals to align with the sponsors' objectives. He emphasized the positive brand exposure and community involvement their support would bring, fostering shared goals.

The struggle continued as he searched for the perfect venue. Negotiating with various event spaces, David proposed flexible dates and co-hosting arrangements, showcasing the potential for increased foot traffic and positive publicity.

Through tenacious negotiation, David secured sponsorships from local businesses and a corporate partner. The sponsors were deeply moved by his dedication and tailored approach. A centrally located venue was secured at a reduced cost, recognizing the event's charitable objectives.

The grand charity event unfolded, with enthusiastic attendees, sponsors, and volunteers coming together to support the cause. Media coverage and social media buzz amplified its impact, leaving a lasting impression on the lives of underprivileged children.

David's story became an inspiring case study on the power of negotiation, even for an ambitious 18-year old. With determination, building relationships, and customizing proposals, he turned his dream into a reality, lighting up the lives of children in his community with hope and education.

What is the Art Of Negotiation?

We will be looking at the meaning of the word "ART" and then "NEGOTIATION" so we can have a deep understanding of the concept.

An **ART** can be seen as a skill that is highly involved; good musicians have good skills, and good footballers also have good skills; the same goes for good negotiators. You can develop a skill so well that it becomes an art.

NEGOTIATION can be seen as a form of discussion between people trying to reach an agreement or gain common ground; when the idea of not settling for less is brought up, negotiation can come into play.

Now let's combine both definitions; the Art of Negotiation means using learned and practised skills to be able to express our thoughts, emotions, and desires in a discussion with others where you are trying to persuade them or get them to change a course of action or see your point of view. The hopeful result is a mutual agreement or at least being able to have the other person or persons see your point of view.

For negotiation to be useful, you have to know what you want; you must be ready to defend your position without fear or flinching.

Having said this much, let's take a look at some practical examples of negotiations in our day-to-day lives.

1. Negotiating with your parents on allowance or college
2. Negotiating with your siblings to help you with your chores
3. Negotiating with your friends about where you should hang out this time
4. Negotiating with yourself to be the best version of yourself
5. Negotiating with your sports coach to allow you to take the lead
6. Negotiating the price of what you are buying from a local vendor

7. Negotiating with your professor about a make-up exam

8. Negotiating to be served better

9. Negotiating with your girlfriend/boyfriend about going to a concert or a movie

I'm sure you can agree that you have experienced a few of the above on the list. Now, here is a big deal, if you don't master the art of negotiation, you won't be able to get the best of it. Imagine being able to tell your parent what you want without them seeing you as a disrespectful young person. Isn't that lovely? Yes, it is.

Now let's talk about some of the benefits of the Art of Negotiation

With the power of negotiation, you can resolve or avoid conflicts that may arise between you and your friends and family. It would be easier for you to resolve issues that may occur without losing a good relationship with the people around you.

Negotiation Skills

Daily, yes every day, we are faced with choices, decisions and challenges, and we must be able to effectively communicate with others in trying to find an acceptable middle ground. I want you to remember that negotiation is a type of communication used to calm disputes and reach an agreement between parties.

Here are some of the vital negotiation skills you need to learn:

Communication: This includes verbal and non-verbal communication skills; these skills are highly required to express yourself in a way that will interest whoever is listening to you. By communicating clearly, you can avoid misunderstandings that might stop you from achieving your desired goal.

With good communication skills, you can talk to parents about what you want and why you want it, and you won't be misunderstood; David understood the communication skills, and that was why he was able to communicate the value that got him to where he wanted to be.

Active listening: this negotiation skill is highly needed to understand the other party's opinion because when it comes to negotiation, you must understand what the other party is saying; active listening helps you pay attention to details to get what the other person is saying.

Emotional intelligence: This is a crucial skill in negotiation; sometimes it will seem as if it is hard to control your emotions, but you must remain calm if you want to be taken seriously. Develop a level of self-awareness on how you show up, and enhance your relationship management skills to recognize others' feelings. Emotional intelligence can allow you to remain focused on the main issue.

Expectation management: In the same way you enter into a negotiation session with a goal, the other party also comes with their own goals. You must be ready to manage your expectations when it comes to negotiation because sometimes, things might not go as planned; you must therefore be prepared to re-strategize and come up with a different plan.

I was told David had lots of rejections when he started his career, but they said the more he was rejected, the more he strategized and came up with a new strategy better than the previous one, and that was why he was able to pull through.

Patience: When it comes to negotiation, be prepared to take time to discuss the details, the pros and cons of different courses of action and to properly assess the situation so that you can come up with the best conclusion. Some negotiations will take longer than expected, especially if the issue being discussed is very intense.

Planning: I love this part so much; negotiations demand extensive planning to figure out what you want; no one should get into a negation discussion without first knowing the desired outcome. You need to plan to come up with your best possible outcome and what you would do if an agreement weren't reached. I told you in the previous skill we discussed, that David was rejected so many times, but each time he was denied, he came up with a new strategy; that is what planning can do for you as a young negotiator.

Persuasion: Hear me, this particular negotiation skill, Is the most essential. Why do you think you were able to accept your friends' point of view on specific issues? It was because of persuasion. They persuaded you to believe them. This particular skill is so vital that many people use it the wrong way to get people scammed; that is to show you how powerful it is.

The reason why no one sees things from your perspective is that you don't persuade enough. Persuasion is simply the ability to influence others to see from your perspective and why your point of view is the ultimate.

Decision-making: Good negotiators are known to be excellent decision-makers. As a negotiator, it hurts your credibility to be seen as drifting all the time, you will have to make a decision and stand by it, no matter the outcome. If you keep changing, then the process has to start over again and again.

Problem-solving: Bear in mind that negotiation will require you to spot the problem, identify why the other party will not agree to your point of view, and together, try to solve it. A solution-finding approach is so very helpful.

Knowing when to walk away. This is the last negotiation skill on this list, and it can be difficult to master. It is essential to enter a negotiation with the knowledge that if there is an impasse or the resolution will compromise your values, then you might need to walk away.

Common Mistakes of Negotiators

Since we have talked more about the skills needed to be a good negotiator, let's talk about some common mistakes to avoid as a young negotiator. I know mistakes are inevitable, but they can be minimized as much as possible: Some mistakes rookie negotiators make are as follows:

- Lack of planning
- Having unrealistic expectations
- Getting overly emotional
- Letting past negative outcomes affect the present ones
- Not knowing when to say no (Accepting too quickly)
- Inability to handle pressure

How to Prepare for a Negotiation

1. Know what you want from the Negotiation
2. Know your values, weaknesses, and strengths
3. Know the lessons to apply from your past negotiations to improve your performance
4. Know the time frame of the Negotiation.
5. Figure out why the other parties will disagree with you so you can anticipate their pushback.

With these few points, I guess you are fired up on how to go about negotiating; when you need to get into an intense discussion with another party, make sure you check all the preparation tips we have discussed.

I want you to go out there and be prepared to negotiate what you need for your life.

Everything is negotiable. Whether or not the negotiation is easy is entirely a different thing
-Carrie Fisher

Extra Credit: 5 Things to Remember

1. Negotiation is a part of life. Sometimes we will have to compromise and meet people halfway to achieve a goal.
2. As much as you are able, try to find what you and the person you are negotiating with have in common.
3. Go into the negotiation process with confidence. If you are not convinced that your perspective is valid, how can you convince someone else?
4. Learn to listen carefully.
5. Practice with someone before you go into the negotiation session.

Chapter 11

SETTING AND ACHIEVING GOALS

As graduation approaches, Maya finds herself feeling overwhelmed by the uncertainties of the future.  She's unsure of her career path, unsure of what she wants to achieve, and unsure her ability to carve out a path for herself. Feeling lost and anxious, Maya turns to her mentor for guidance on setting and achieving meaningful goals that will empower her to navigate the journey ahead. It is normal when someone is finished with high school, to have dreams, and setting goals is the best way to be able to work on these dreams for your life. Going a step further, actually achieving these goals can make a difference between feeling successful or feeling stagnant.

Setting goals involves identifying specific objectives or outcomes that you want to accomplish within a certain timeframe. These goals serve as a roadmap for success, providing direction, motivation, and focus as you work towards realizing your dreams.

Benefits of setting goals

- Provides clarity and direction in life
- Increases your motivation and focus
- Boosts your self-confidence and self-esteem
- Facilitates your personal growth and development
- Enhances your problem-solving and decision-making skills
- Gives you a sense of achievement when they are accomplished

Here are ten (10) tips to help you with setting and achieving goals:

1. Reflect on your values and passions: Take time to identify what truly matters to you and what you're passionate about. Even though you listen to parents and

friends, also listen to your own heart. Align your goals with your values and interests to ensure they click with your authentic self.

2. Set SMART goals: Ensure your goals are Specific, Measurable, Achievable, Relevant, and Time-bound. Break down larger goals into smaller, actionable steps to make them more manageable and attainable.

Specific: *This means your goal should be super clear and to the point. Instead of saying, "I want to get better at math," you could say, "I want to improve my math grade by two letter grades."*

Measurable: *Your goal should be something you can measure, so you know when you've reached it. Like, if you're trying to save money, saying, "I want to save $500 by the end of the year" is better than just saying, "I want to save some money."*

Achievable: *Your goal should be something you can actually do. It's cool to dream big, but it's also important to be realistic. If you're not the best at basketball, setting a goal to play in the NBA next year might not be very achievable.*

Relevant: *Your goal should be something that matters to you and fits in with what you want to do. If you love writing,* *setting a goal to start a blog might be super relevant and exciting for you.*

Time-bound: *This means giving yourself a deadline. Instead of saying, "I want to learn to play the guitar someday," you could say, "I want to learn three songs on the guitar by the end of the summer."*

1. Create a vision board: Visualize your goals by creating a vision board filled with pictures, quotes, memes and affirmations that represent what you hope to achieve. Display it somewhere visible to keep your goals at the forefront of your mind.

2. Develop an action plan: Outline the steps required to achieve each goal, including deadlines and milestones. Break down tasks into smaller, manageable chunks and prioritize them based on importance and how soon you want to accomplish them.

3. Keep track of your progress: From time to time, bring out your goal book or App or whatever you are using and review and evaluate your progress towards your goals. Celebrate your successes and adjust your approach as needed to overcome obstacles and stay on track.

4. Visualize success: Take time each day to visualize yourself achieving your goals. Imagine the emotions, sensations, and experiences associated with accomplishing your objectives. Visualization can help reinforce your commitment and keep you motivated when you feel down, lazy, or just tired.

5. Break goals into bite-sized tasks: So, you know when you have a big goal, like passing college entry exams. Instead of looking at the whole mountain you have to climb, you focus on one step at a time. You could study one chapter a night or make flashcards. Taking it one step at a time makes it way less overwhelming, trust me!

6. Stay organized: Keeping track of your goals is like having a secret weapon to help you stay on top of things! Use a planner, journal, or digital tools to write down your goals, set reminders, and track your progress. Set deadlines and check-ins to stay accountable and organized. With a little organization, you'll be unstoppable!

7. Look at failure as feedback: You know how sometimes things don't go as planned? Well, guess what? That's totally normal. Everyone faces setbacks and failures on the journey to success. But

here's the thing – instead of letting failure bring you down, see it as a chance to learn and grow. Every setback is like a little bump in the road that teaches you something new.

8. Review and revise regularly: Life happens and often, things change. It's super important to check your progress regularly to see how you're doing. Take a look at what's working and what's not, and don't be afraid to make some changes if you need to. Being flexible and adaptable is key to staying on track and making sure you're still headed in the right direction.

Setting goals is the first step in turning the invisible into the visible. - Tony Robbins

By the way, have you ever heard of the **WOOP** tool for goal setting? It's pretty cool and super practical – perfect for helping you tackle those big dreams you've got brewing. Here's the lowdown:

WISH - First things first! Think about what you really want to achieve. It could be anything from boosting your grades to starting a new workout routine or sharpening up your communication skills. Make sure your wish is clear and totally meaningful to you.

OUTCOME - Once you've got your wish locked in, picture what success would look like. Imagine yourself acing that test, crushing your workout, or nailing that presentation. Visualize all the awesome feelings that come with achieving your goal.

OBSTACLE - Now, let's get real – what might stand in your way? Think about anything that could trip you up, like running out of time, feeling unmotivated, or not having the right resources. Being honest about potential roadblocks helps you plan ahead.

PLAN - Time to make a game plan! Break down your goal into smaller steps and figure out how to tackle those obstacles head-on. Set deadlines, make to-do lists, and get ready to hustle. Having a solid plan in place sets you up for success.

The WOOP tool is all about finding that balance between dreaming big and being practical. It helps you set goals that are both ambitious and totally doable, so you can make your dreams a reality. Ready to WOOP it up and crush those goals? Let's do this!

And here's the cool part about setting and achieving goals – every time you finish one, you celebrate! It's like a mini victory dance. Whether it's treating yourself to your favorite snack or taking a break to hang out with friends, celebrating each win keeps you motivated and pumped to keep going.

So, for all the things you want in this life, it might seem like a mountain now, but just make a plan, get support, follow the techniques we have talked about, and work at it with everything you've got, asking for help when you need it. Here's to becoming the awesome person you're meant to be!

You've got this!

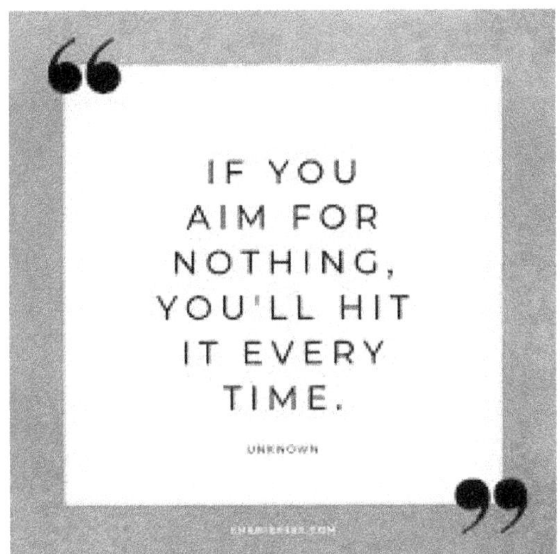

Extra Credit Tips

1. Cultivate a Growth Mindset: Don't let difficulties stop you. Instead, embrace challenges and setbacks as opportunities for growth and learning.

2. Stay Flexible: As much as possible, be open to adjusting your goals and plans as circumstances change or new opportunities arise.

3. Ask for help: Lean on supportive family, mentors, and friends who can offer guidance, encouragement, and resources when needed.

4. Practice Self-Compassion: Be kind to yourself and recognize that setbacks and failures are part of the journey towards success.

5. Celebrate Progress: Acknowledge and celebrate each milestone and achievement along the way to keep yourself motivated and inspired.

Chapter 12

CHOOSING A CAREER

As a child Christine always dreamed of becoming a teacher. Every year for as long as she could remember she always chose to be a teacher at career day and dressed the part. She loved Mrs.  Ruby who was her favourite teacher and wished that she could grow up to be just like her. When Christine started middle school her dreams of becoming a teacher was still there but the feeling wasn't as strong as it was in her pre-school days. It was nearing graduation and college applications were soon to be sent out. When browsing for the right college, Christine's mom asked, "Still wanna be a teacher"? At that point, Christine started to realize that her dream career as a child was no longer what she really wanted to do. In fact, she was unsure of the path she really wanted to take now that the time had come for her to choose her career path.

The next day Christine went to her friend Zoey and asked her what she was planning on doing after high school. Zoey said that she thought she wanted to be a doctor but it was only because her parents suggested it and they already started making plans for her to study to become a doctor. Zoey said she didn't want to disappoint her parents so she was going along with their decision. Christine and Zoey decided to go to their school counsellor for some advice on choosing the right career. The counsellor told them that choosing a career should be a personal choice and the best way to begin the career process is to know what skills they may have, their personalities and their interest. The counsellor gave them an assignment to simply start observing themselves and in a week they should return with the fascinating results they found. The girls were not as confused as before but were aimed at discovering themselves and the career that they would decide to choose.

Making the Choice on Your Career

Choosing a career can feel like stepping into a maze—there are many options and different persons might be suggesting different things. You yourself might not even be sure of the direction you want to go in. However, as confusing as it might be, the decision to choose a career is one of the most crucial and exciting journeys you will embark upon Discovering your passions, talents and interests is key to making informed decisions that set the stage for a satisfying and rewarding career.

It's also very important to understand this does not have to be a lifelong decision that can never be changed, it's just the basic step that is taken when you finish high school. Many persons have made a switch later on and it turned out pretty well. The idea is to at least start something.

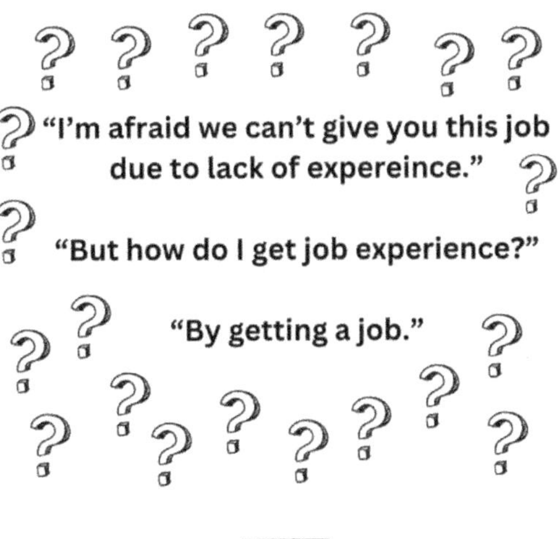

The Secrets to Choosing a Career

#1 Know Yourself

Before you dive headfirst into the sea of career options, take a moment to know yourself. What are your passions, interests, and strengths? What makes you come alive? Think about the activities that you lose track of time doing—the ones that make your heart dance with joy. These clues are like breadcrumbs that lead you to your true calling.

#2 Seek Guidance

Don't be shy to reach out for help and guidance. Talk to your parents, teachers, or trusted mentors. Seek advice from professionals in the fields you're considering. Ask questions about their journeys, challenges, and what they love about their jobs. Their insights can offer valuable perspectives and may help you see things from new angles.

#3 Embrace Failure

Sometimes, you'll make a career choice that doesn't work out as planned. Embrace failure as a steppingstone, not a roadblock. Every setback is an opportunity to learn, grow, and discover what truly ignites your passion. The road to success isn't always a straight line—embrace the twists and turns as part of your unique journey.

#4 Follow Your Heart, But Keep Your Eyes Open

When choosing a career, listen to your heart, but don't forget to keep your eyes open too. Passion is essential, but it's also crucial to consider practical aspects like job market demand, salary potential, and work-life balance. Striking a balance between passion and pragmatism can lead you to a fulfilling and sustainable career.

#5 Embrace Flexibility

In today's rapidly changing world, careers are more fluid than ever before. Embrace the idea of flexibility and continuous learning. Be open to adapting and evolving as you discover new interests and opportunities along your journey. Your career path might take unexpected turns, and that's okay—it's all part of the adventure.

#6 Take Your Time

Choosing a career is a significant decision, and it's okay to take your time. There's no rush to have it all figured out by a certain age. Allow yourself to explore and discover. Trust that the right path will unfold at the right time. Remember, it's not about finding the perfect career but embracing a career that allows you to grow and thrive.

Mastering Self-Discovery

Self-discovery is very important when deciding which career to choose. There is no better time than now if you have not already figured out who you are than now. Understanding yourself and your passions will make the choice of what you decide to dedicate your time and energy to worthwhile. Not only will it help you choose your intended profession, but it will allow you to learn things about yourself that you may have overlooked. Sometimes life becomes so routine that we forget to reflect on ourselves and what we are doing with our lives.

Choosing a career is a big step and it would be great if there were ways that you could apply to this transition to make it easy and not an overwhelming feeling of despair. Reflecting on your interests, strengths, and values are at the top of the list. This will allow you to be more aware of yourself and begin unleashing your passions, exploring hobbies and extracurricular activities that spark joy in your life.

Several things should be done when you have thrown your graduation hat in the air in celebration of your completion of high-school. This checklist will help you cross out the things that you should keep in mind to help you on your route to the world of work where you will be bringing in your finances and learning to collaborate and work along with others while being successful in your career path.

> "Your career is like a garden. It can hold an assortment of life's energy that yields a bounty for you. You do not need to grow just one thing in your garden. You do not need to do just one thing in your career."
>
> —Jennifer Ritchie Payette

Choosing a Career To-Do List

Identify your strengths: Using your skills and natural talents to make the right career choices is a way to work smart, not hard. This will be beneficial when you have entered the workforce and allow you to provide quality service.

☐ Explore Career Options: Broaden your horizons by discovering a vast array of career paths and industries. Investigating emerging fields and technological advancements by checking out in-demand careers of the future will give you perspective of the various career choices.

☐ Research and Gather Information: Research potential careers to find the best fit for your aspirations and understand job roles and responsibilities. Utilize career counselors, online tools, and informational interviews. Building connections to gain valuable insights into different professions. Evaluating educational requirements: Understanding the academic qualifications needed for your chosen career.

☐ Overcome Challenges and Limiting Beliefs: Dealing with societal expectations and breaking free from traditional career norms can be a struggle. You can start embracing your individuality by setting your trends and looking within yourself for inspiration. Facing fear and uncertainty is a stepping stone to success. Overcoming gender and cultural biases, challenging stereotypes to pursue your dream career are steps that should be taken so you can have the healthiest experience when you have made your choice.

☐ Gaining Practical Experience: Real-world experience through internships and part-time jobs strengthens your resume. It also helps you see the real deal when it comes to working in certain areas and the challenges and opportunities that each career comes with. You can contribute by doing volunteer work and community involvement contributing to causes you care about while building skills is the way a productive leader behaves. Create a portfolio while you're at it. Showcase your talents and accomplishments to potential employers.

☐ Decision-Making and Setting Goals: Setting SMART goals is the way to go. You can start by creating a clear roadmap to achieve your career aspirations. Finding the intersection between your interests and job market demands will help you balance your passion and practicality. Trusting your intuition and confidence in your career choices will be the final decision.

Your first career choice does not have to be your last. That is why volunteering to gain experience is very important and will work to your advantage. When you do this, you will have started learning the art of embracing change and recognizing the potential for career shifts throughout your life. Reskilling and upskilling will allow you to prepare for career changes and adapt to new opportunities. This is the perfect time to find purpose and fulfilment, seeking personal growth and job satisfaction throughout your career is something that might take a while to discover, so while you are on your journey ensure to learn from your experiences and make them work to your advantage.

Conclusion

As you navigate the career maze, remember that choosing a career is not about finding a final destination—it's about embracing the journey. It's about knowing yourself, exploring your options, seeking guidance, and being open to growth. Embrace the uncertainty, stay true to your passions, and trust that you have the power to create a career that fills you with joy and purpose. Trust yourself—you've got this! "You've already taken the first step towards a rewarding career journey. Remember, choosing a career is not a one-time decision; it's a lifelong adventure of self-discovery, growth, and adaptation. Embrace your unique talents, passions, and dreams as you explore the vast world of career possibilities. Stay curious, remain resilient, and never stop learning. Your future is yours to create, and this guide has armed you with the tools to make informed decisions that lead you to a fulfilling and purpose-driven career. Happy career exploration!

Extra Credit: 5 Things to Remember

1. Your first career choice does not have to be your last, you can change it when you learn more about yourself and the work that fits you best.

2. It's okay to ask for help when picking a career path, you can seek help from an older person you trust.

3. Self-discovery is one of the most important and simple ways of choosing a career.

4. Volunteering is one of the best ways to get experience when you have decided on a career.

5. Exploring different career options will help you to know what type of career opportunities are available.

Chapter 13

BUILDING SELF-CONFIDENCE

As Sarah stepped onto the stage to deliver her valedictorian speech, her heart pounded against her chest. Doubts crept into her mind – What if she stumbled over her words? What if nobody

listened? Yet, as she began to speak, she felt a surge of confidence wash over her. With each word, she realized the power of self-belief and the impact it could have on her success.

Self-confidence is like a superpower that allows us to face challenges, pursue our dreams, and conquer the world. As you embark on this new chapter of your life after high school, building and nurturing your self-confidence will be essential for navigating the ups and downs that lie ahead.

Self-confidence is not about being perfect or never feeling fear. Instead, it's about trusting yourself, embracing your strengths, and believing in your ability to overcome obstacles. It's the inner voice that whispers, "You've got this" when doubt creeps in.

The way to develop self-confidence is to do the thing you fear and get a record of successful experiences behind you. - William Jennings Bryan

Here are ten (10) ways to grow your self-confidence superpowers:

1. Embrace Your Unique Qualities

Celebrate what makes you different and special. Remember, your quirks and imperfections are what make you stand out from the crowd.

2. Set Realistic Goals

Break down your goals into manageable steps and celebrate your progress along the way. Every small victory is a testament to your capabilities.

3. Practice Self-Compassion

Be kind to yourself, especially when things don't go as planned. Treat yourself with the same kindness and understanding that you would offer to a friend facing a challenge. Confidence does not mean you have to be perfect.

4. Step Out of Your Comfort Zone

Growth happens when we push ourselves beyond our comfort zones. Whether it's trying something new or taking on a challenge, each step outside your comfort zone strengthens your confidence muscles.

5. Surround Yourself with Positivity

Choose to spend time with people who lift you up and encourage you to be your best self. Avoid those who drain your energy or undermine your confidence.

6. Focus on Your Strengths

Identify your strengths and talents, and make a conscious effort to focus on them. When faced with challenges, remind yourself of past successes and the unique qualities that have helped you overcome obstacles in the past.

7. Practice Visualization

Visualize yourself succeeding in various situations, whether it's giving a presentation, acing an interview, or making new friends. Imagining yourself achieving your goals can help boost your confidence and reduce anxiety when faced with real-life scenarios.

8. Seek Feedback and Learn from Mistakes

Don't be afraid to seek feedback from others, whether it's from mentors, teachers, or peers. Constructive criticism can help you identify areas for improvement and growth as an individual. Similarly, view mistakes as learning opportunities rather than failures, and use them as stepping stones toward personal growth.

9. Set Boundaries and Say No

Learn to assert yourself and set boundaries with others. Saying no to things that don't align with your values or priorities is an important aspect of self-care and self-respect. Prioritize your well-being and don't be afraid to advocate for yourself.

10. Practice Gratitude

Cultivate an attitude of gratitude by focusing on the positive aspects of your life. Take time each day to reflect on what you're grateful for, whether it's supportive friends and family, personal accomplishments, or simple pleasures. Gratitude can help shift your mindset from one of self-doubt to one of self-assurance and appreciation.

The importance of positive Self-Talk in Building Confidence

Sometimes I know as young people, you listen to the 'Tiktok' influencers, friends, and other persons. However, self-talk plays an important role in building confidence as it directly influences our beliefs, attitudes, and behaviors. The conversations we have with ourselves, whether positive or negative, shape our self-perception and ultimately impact how we approach challenges and opportunities.

Positive self-talk involves affirming statements that encourage self-belief, resilience, and optimism, while negative self-talk can erode confidence and breed self-doubt. Examples of positive self-talk are:

"I can do all things through Christ who gives me strength"

"I make mistakes but I will keep improving"

"I believe in myself"

By cultivating a habit of positive self-talk, you can challenge the thoughts that make you feel weak and inadequate, you can boost your self-esteem, and foster a mindset of growth and possibilities. Through constructive and empowering internal dialogue, you can cultivate a sense of self-assurance, overcome setbacks with resilience, and pursue your goals with greater confidence and determination.

Strengths Inventory Worksheet

Here are some exercises that will help you as you seek to boost your confidence levels. Reflect on your experiences, achievements, and challenges to identify your strengths, talents, and areas for growth.

Circle the strengths that resonate with you.

1. Strengths:

- Creativity   - Adaptability

- Leadership   - Resilience

- Problem-solving   - Teamwork

- Communication   - Organization

- Empathy   - Perseverance

- Other: _______________________________________

2. Talents/Skills:

List activities or tasks that come naturally to you or that you excel at. This could include hobbies, sports, academic subjects, or creative pursuits.

1. _________________   2. _________________

3. _________________   4. _________________

5. _________________   6. _________________

7. _________________   8. _________________

9. _________________   10. _________________

3. Areas for Growth:

Identify areas where you may want to improve or develop further. This could include skills you admire in others, areas you find challenging, or goals you want to pursue.

1. _________________   2. _________________

3. _________________   4. _________________

5. _________________   6. _________________

7. _________________   8. _________________

9. _________________   10. _________________

4. Values and Passions:

Reflect on your values, passions, and long-term aspirations. Consider how your strengths and talents align with your values and how you can use these qualities to pursue your passions and goals.

____

____

____

____

____

Reflection Questions:

1. What strengths do you feel most confident about?
2. How can you leverage your strengths to overcome challenges?
3. Which talents or skills are you most excited to further develop?

4. What steps can you take to address areas for growth?

5. How do your strengths align with your values and passions?

6. What goals can you set based on your strengths and talents?

Action Plan

Based on your reflections, create an action plan for further developing your strengths and addressing areas for growth. Set specific, measurable, achievable, relevant, and time-bound (SMART) goals to guide your progress.

Remember: Building self-awareness takes time and reflection. Be patient with yourself as you explore your strengths and areas for growth, and celebrate your progress along the way!

Conclusion

Remember, developing self-confidence is a journey that takes time and effort. Be patient with yourself, celebrate your progress, and continue to invest in your personal growth and development. With dedication and perseverance, you can build the self-confidence needed to thrive in all aspects of your life.

As you make the transition from high school to adulthood, remember that self-confidence is a skill that can be cultivated and strengthened over time. By embracing your unique qualities, setting realistic goals, practicing self-compassion, stepping out of your comfort zone, and surrounding yourself with positivity, you can build the self-confidence needed to thrive in the world beyond the classroom. So, stand tall, believe in yourself, and let your confidence shine!

Extra Credit

1. Keep a "Confidence Journal" where you record your achievements, big or small, and reflect on moments when you felt proud of yourself.

2. Practice positive affirmations daily. Repeat phrases like "I am capable," "I am worthy," and "I believe in myself" to reinforce your self-confidence.

3. Seek out opportunities to volunteer or help others. Making a positive impact on someone else's life can boost your own self-esteem.

4. Take care of your physical health by getting enough sleep, exercising regularly, and nourishing your body with healthy food. A healthy body contributes to a healthy mind.

5. Remember, self-confidence is a journey, not a destination. Be patient with yourself and trust that with time and effort, you will continue to grow and flourish.

Chapter 14

HANDLING CONFLICT

In the lively school halls of Oakridge High, Jake found himself caught in the middle of a heated dispute between two friends, Sarah and Max. The tension escalated over a misunderstanding about a group project and was threatening to fracture their longtime friendship.

Rather than taking sides, Jake decided to mediate the situation. He invited Sarah and Max to a quiet corner of the school courtyard, providing a neutral space for open communication. With empathy, he encouraged each of them to express their feelings and perspectives.

Listening attentively, Jake helped them see the situation from each other's point of view. He facilitated a constructive dialogue, focusing on finding common ground. Through this process, they discovered that miscommunication and assumptions fueled the conflict.

Together, they brainstormed solutions and agreed on a plan to improve communication within their group. Jake played a crucial role in fostering understanding and unity. As a result, the trio not only resolved their immediate conflict but also strengthened their bond, learning valuable lessons about effective communication and teamwork.

When navigating life's toughest test there is one skill that's bound to come in handy to help and it is conflict resolution. If you haven't realized it already, life is full of conflicts, whether they're with friends, family, coworkers, or even within yourself. Learning how to resolve conflicts is like acquiring a superpower that can make your journey through life smoother and more fulfilling. In this chapter, we'll delve into the art of conflict resolution in a way that's easy to understand and practical to apply.

The Nature of Conflict

You may all be aware that conflict exists, but do you know where it comes from and why it exists.

What is the Nature of Conflict?

Before we dive into resolving conflicts, let's understand what they are and why they happen. Conflict isn't necessarily a bad thing; it's a natural part of life. It occurs when people have differing views, needs, or expectations. You'll find yourself in conflicts more often than you'd like, but it's how you deal with them that matters. There are so many people existing in this world with different personalities, characters, likes and dislikes so having conflict would be something that naturally occurs because of the difference in people. Let's say your annual family vacation is coming up and a decision of where to travel is put to each family member, there's a choice between Antigua and Barbuda or Italy. Family members have chosen their destination, but the choice is even two members have chosen Antigua and Barbuda and the other two chose Italy. This is an example of how easy a conflicting situation can happen.

Another important thing to know about conflict is the type of conflict you are faced with. There are different types of conflicts, and it's essential to identify which type you're facing. Here are a few common ones:

- Interpersonal Conflicts: These are personal disputes between individuals. They can be with friends, family, or significant others.
- Intrapersonal Conflicts: These are inner battles, where you're in conflict with yourself. It often involves conflicting emotions, values, or goals.
- Inter-group Conflicts: These occur when entire groups or communities have opposing interests. Think of rival sports teams or political parties.
- Workplace Conflicts: Common in professional settings, these arise when colleagues, managers, or employees have disagreements related to work tasks, decisions, or expectations.
- Societal Conflicts: These encompass larger societal issues, like political disputes or social injustices.

The Causes of Conflict

Conflicts may occur every day, several times a day; whether it's conflict within yourself battling with a major decision you need to make in your life, like what career should you choose to go after when you have completed high school or if you should continue being friends with someone that makes you feel bad about yourself.

Understanding the root causes of conflict is vital for effective resolution. This would mean that you would have to be open minded about the situation and not go off of your feelings. There are many different reasons that you will experience conflict and it will make it so much easier for you to resolve it if you know what caused it. Like any problem, knowing the source of the issue allows you to know the best way to make the situation better.

These are the most common ways conflicts can stem:

Miscommunication: Often, conflicts arise from misunderstandings or a lack of effective communication. As a recent high school graduate, you'll appreciate how simple misunderstandings can escalate into significant conflicts.

Unmet Expectations: When people have different expectations about a situation or a relationship, conflict can emerge.

Scarce Resources: Competition for limited resources like time, money, or opportunities can lead to conflicts.

Different Values and Beliefs: Differing worldviews can cause clashes. This often happens in inter-group and societal conflicts.

The Building Blocks of Conflict Resolution

Having and implementing the building blocks of conflict resolution is crucial for several reasons. It promotes a healthy work or personal environment by preventing prolonged disputes, enhancing relationships, and fostering collaboration. Effective conflict resolution also improves communication skills, builds trust among individuals, and contributes to a more positive and productive atmosphere. Ultimately, it ensures that conflicts are addressed constructively, leading to better problem-solving and overall team cohesion.

Building blocks are set in place to construct a strong foundation so that when any disturbances come along, you can be stable and not get thrown off by a heavy wind of conflict or maybe even a hurricane or tsunami storm of conflict.

Follow these guidelines and when conflicts come your way you will be able to deal with them like a pro.

1. Understand That Conflict Is Normal

First things first, conflict is not the enemy; it's a normal part of life. It's like rain—it's going to happen. Even the most peaceful people have conflicts. So, don't fear it; embrace it as a chance to learn, grow, and build stronger relationships.

2. Choose Your Battles

Not every conflict is worth your energy. It's crucial to differentiate between a trivial disagreement and an issue that truly matters. Before diving into the fray, ask yourself:

"Is this worth my time and emotional investment?" Sometimes, it's best to let things slide.

3. Listen Actively

When conflict arises, don't just wait for your turn to speak. Truly listen to the other person's perspective. Listening actively shows respect, and it can also unveil insights you might have missed.

4. Take a Breather

In the heat of a dispute, emotions can run high. If you feel like you're about to boil over, it's okay to take a break. Excuse yourself, go for a walk, take deep breaths, or do something that calms you. Returning to the conversation when you're both cooler-headed can lead to a more productive dialogue.

5. Seek Compromise

Often, conflicts can be resolved through compromise. Both parties may have to give a little to find common ground. It's not about winning or losing; it's about finding a solution that works for everyone.

6. Learn to Apologize

We all make mistakes. Knowing how to apologize is a vital skill. When you're in the wrong, own up to it, express your regret, and show your commitment to making amends.

7. Embrace Differences

Remember, everyone is unique. You won't always agree with others, and that's perfectly fine. Embrace diversity in opinions, values, and perspectives. It's what makes the world an interesting place.

8. Seek Mediation if Necessary

In some cases, conflicts can become deeply entrenched and seem impossible to resolve. In such situations, seeking a mediator—a neutral third party—can help facilitate communication and guide you towards a resolution.

9. Learn and Grow

Every conflict, whether big or small, holds a lesson. After it's resolved, take a moment to reflect on what you've learned. Did you gain new insights about yourself or the other person? Did you discover better ways to communicate or handle disputes? Use these lessons to grow as an individual.

10. Practice Self-Care

Managing conflicts can be emotionally draining. Make self-care a priority. Whether it's engaging in a hobby, spending time with loved ones, or practicing mindfulness, take care of your mental and emotional well-being.

11. Build a Support System

Don't tackle conflicts alone. Lean on your support system—friends, family, mentors, or a therapist. They can offer guidance, lend a listening ear, and remind you that you're not alone in your struggles.

12. Let Go of Grudges

Holding onto grudges only weighs you down. Learn to forgive, not necessarily for the other person's benefit, but for your peace of mind. It's like decluttering your emotional space.

13. Remember, You're Growing

As high school graduates, you're at a pivotal point in your lives. You're learning, evolving, and discovering your place in the world. Along the way, you'll encounter plenty of bumps and roadblocks. Keep in mind that conflicts are a part of your growth journey. They're stepping stones that shape your character, wisdom, and resilience.

The Art of Conflict Resolution

Art is not only a physical representation of beauty and dynamic dimensions, it is more than a drawing or a painting or even a stone sculpture, art can also be described as the strategic way that someone handles a situation.

Understanding how to develop the art of conflict resolution will allow you to turn any situation into a beautiful masterpiece of keeping our cool and making the best outcome out of a rocky and forbidden path.

Now, let's explore practical steps to navigate the maze of conflict resolution.

Keep Calm and Listen

When conflicts heat up, the first step is to stay calm. Emotions can cloud judgment, so take a deep breath and focus on listening actively. Give the other party the opportunity to express their concerns without interruptions. This shows respect and helps to understand their perspective.

Put Yourself in Their Shoes

Empathy is a powerful tool in conflict resolution. Try to see the situation from the other person's point of view. Understanding their feelings and needs can make it easier to find a middle ground.

Use "I" Statements

When it's your turn to express yourself, use "I" statements to convey your feelings and concerns without blaming or accusing. For example, say, "I felt hurt when..." instead of "You hurt me when..."

Seek Common Ground

Look for areas where you both agree or share common goals. This common ground can serve as a foundation for finding a compromise.

Brainstorm Solutions

Once you've understood each other's perspectives, work together to brainstorm solutions. Be open to new ideas and be willing to find creative ways to address the issue.

Choose Your Battles

Not every conflict needs to be resolved immediately. As a recent graduate, you'll learn that some things are best left alone, while others require attention. Decide which conflicts are worth your time and energy.

Conflict Resolution in Real Life

Thinking about how we should and will handle a situation sometimes turns out different from the way we actually handle the situation. We may think that we would say and do this when the time arrives but because it may not happen exactly how we played it out in our heads and sometimes are not bold enough to say or do what we planned the situation turns out differently. Or it could be that our emotions got the best of us, and we go off the path of resolving the situation and become engulfed by what the person says or does.

This is quite common and if it happens you can use it as a learning experience for the next time a conflicting situation comes. There are ways that you can keep track of the way you are dealing with the situation and if you think you are being derailed there are ways to get back on track. There are certain principles that can be used in various situations that can keep you in charge and in control of your emotions.

Now, let's apply these principles to real-life situations.

Conflict with Friends or Roommates

Living with friends or roommates can be exciting, but it can also lead to conflicts over shared spaces, responsibilities, or different schedules. Here's how to handle it:

Listen: When a dispute arises, listen to your friends or roommates without interrupting.

Empathize: Understand their needs and feelings. Maybe they're stressed or tired, and it's affecting their behavior.

Share Your Perspective: Calmly express how their actions or decisions affect you. Use "I" statements.

Brainstorm Solutions: Work together to find compromises. Maybe you can set clear boundaries or create a shared calendar.

Conflict with Family

Family conflicts are a part of growing up. Whether it's disagreements about curfew, chores, or personal boundaries, handling family conflicts can be challenging. Here's what you can do:

Stay Calm: Emotions can run high but try to stay calm and respectful.

Seek Common Ground: Find shared values or goals. You all want a harmonious home, after all.

Use Empathy: Understand your parents' or siblings' perspectives, even if you don't agree.

Discuss and Compromise: Engage in open discussions and find solutions that work for everyone.

Conclusion

Conflict resolution is a valuable skill that will serve you well as you step into the world after high school. Remember, conflicts are a part of life, but how you approach them makes all the difference. By staying calm, listening actively, and seeking common ground, you can navigate the maze of conflict resolution with grace and confidence.

Don't fear conflict; embrace it as an opportunity for personal and interpersonal growth. Your journey post-graduation will be filled with ups and downs, but each conflict you face can be a stepping stone toward becoming the best version of yourself. So, chin up, and get ready to navigate life's toughest tests with wisdom and grace. Your future is bright, and you've got what it takes to shine!

Chapter 15

MANAGING

YOUR DIGITAL PRESENCE

I magine this: You're chatting with friends online, scrolling through your social media feeds, and exploring the joys of the internet. Everything seems fun and exciting until you 

stumble upon a suspicious link or receive a friend request from a stranger who seems much older. Suddenly, you're faced with a dilemma – how do you stay safe and protect your privacy in this digital jungle?

Welcome to the world of technology, where the possibilities are endless, but so are the risks. In this chapter, we'll dive deep into the realm of online safety, privacy, and digital responsibility. From safeguarding your personal information to avoiding cyber threats, we'll equip you with the knowledge and skills you need to navigate the digital landscape with confidence and caution.

We need the internet – we can't get away from how important it is. From keeping up-to-date on current events to filling out our job applications to doing research for colleges, etc. We spend time on it daily, so let's figure out how to use it responsibly and safely.

Use strong passwords

Create passwords that are hard for others to guess but easy for you to remember. Avoid using obvious combinations like "123456" or your birthdate. A strong password has a mix of letters, numbers, and symbols, making it tougher for hackers to crack.

Think before you share

Be careful with what you post online. Once it's out there, it's hard to take it back. Avoid sharing personal information like your address, phone number, or school name with people you don't know in real life. Think twice before posting photos or videos that could be embarrassing or harmful.

Keep your privacy settings tight

Most social media platforms have privacy settings that let you control who sees your posts and personal info. Take advantage of these settings to keep your profile private or limit who can see your posts. Regularly review and update your privacy settings to stay in control of your digital presence.

Be wary of strangers

Not everyone online is who he or she claims to be. Be cautious when interacting with people you don't know, especially if they ask for personal information or try to meet up in person. Trust your instincts and don't hesitate to block or report anyone who makes you uncomfortable to a parent or .other responsible person.

Avoid cyberbullying

Cyberbullying is never okay. Treat others online with kindness and respect, just as you would in real life. Don't engage in hurtful behavior like spreading rumors, sending mean messages, or posting hurtful comments. If you witness cyberbullying, speak up and report it to a trusted adult or authority figure.

Think before you click

Be careful when clicking on links or downloading files from unknown sources. They could contain viruses that can harm your device or steal your personal information. If something seems suspicious or too good to be true, it's best to err on the side of caution and avoid clicking.

Protect your devices

Keep your devices secure by installing antivirus software and keeping them up-to-date with the latest security patches. Avoid downloading apps or software from unofficial sources, as they may contain malware or spyware. Lock your devices with a PIN or password to prevent unauthorized access.

Be Mindful of your digital footprint

Everything you do online leaves a digital footprint. Be mindful of what you post, comment on, or share, as it can impact your reputation and future opportunities. Employers and colleges often check applicants' social media profiles, so think about how you want to present yourself online.

Be a responsible digital citizen

Take responsibility for your actions online and think about the impact they have on others. Use technology for good, whether it's by spreading positivity, raising awareness about important issues, or supporting your community. Be a role model for others and help create a safer, more respectful online environment for everyone.

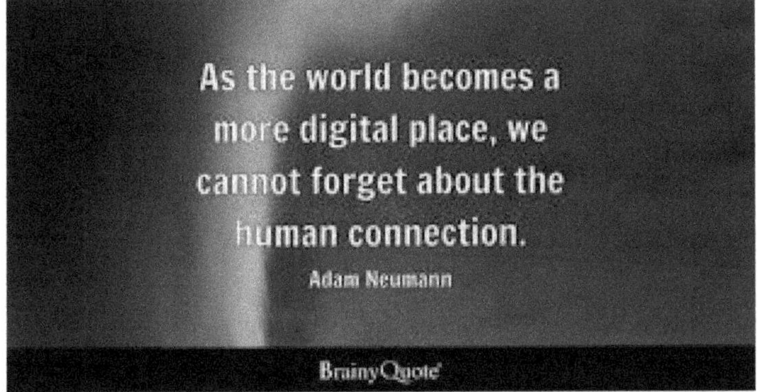

By the way....How could we talk about the digital world and not talk about **AI (Artificial Intelligence)**

AI is like a super-smart computer system that can do some things humans can do, like learn from information, make decisions, and even talk to us like a friend. You've probably seen it in action with virtual assistants like Siri or Alexa, or when Netflix suggests movies you might like based on what you've watched before. While AI can be helpful, here are some guidelines for its use:

Be mindful of your limits: Using AI for schoolwork can be incredibly helpful, but it's essential to use it responsibly and not let it be a substitute for your own creativity. Use it to generate ideas, but make sure the final work is your own. Don't just copy and paste what AI gives, but take the time to read, understand, and edit/paraphrase the material in your own words.

Use Multiple Sources: Don't rely only on AI-generated content for your research. Seek out a variety of sources, including books, articles, and reputable websites, to ensure that you're getting a well-rounded understanding of your topic.

Use AI for Good: AI has the potential to do amazing things, such as diagnosing diseases or solving complex problems. Get involved in projects or activities that use AI for positive change, like helping the environment or supporting social justice causes.

Stay curious, stay informed, and use AI for good!

Digital Use and Health

Let's chat about something super important - how our devices affect our physical and mental health. We all love our cell phones, tablets, and computers, right? They keep us connected, entertained, and informed. But it's essential to remember that too much screen time can have some not-so-good effects on our bodies and minds.

First, let's talk about physical health. Spending too much time hunched over our devices can lead to neck and back pain, eye strain, and headaches. It's essential to take regular breaks, stretch, and practice good posture to avoid these issues. Try to limit screen time before bed too, as the blue light from screens can mess with your sleep and leave you feeling tired and groggy the next day.

Now, onto mental health. While our devices can be a source of entertainment and connection, they can also contribute to stress, anxiety, and even depression. Scrolling through social media can sometimes make us feel as if we're not good enough or that everyone else has a perfect life. Remember, what we see online isn't always the full picture, and it's essential to take breaks and focus on real-life connections and activities that make us happy.

So, what can you do to keep yourself healthy and happy while still enjoying your devices?

First, try to set limits on screen time. It can be tempting to spend hours glued to our screens, but it's essential to take breaks and give our minds and bodies a rest.

Next, make sure you're using your devices in ways that make you feel good. Follow positive accounts, engage in meaningful conversations, and take breaks when you start to feel overwhelmed.

Finally, remember to prioritize self-care. Get outside, exercise, spend time with friends and family, and do activities that make you feel good about yourself. And if you ever start to feel overwhelmed or anxious, don't hesitate to reach out for help. There are plenty of resources and support networks available to help you figure out the ups and downs of device use and mental health. For example, www.commonsensemedia.org.

By mastering the art of online safety, privacy, and digital responsibility, you'll not only protect yourself from harm but also contribute to a safer and more secure internet environment for everyone. So, keep these tips in mind as you navigate the digital world, and remember – stay savvy, stay safe!

Extra Credit Tips:

1. Keep your software and devices up to date to patch security vulnerabilities.
2. Enable two-factor authentication for an extra layer of protection on your accounts.

3. Educate yourself about common online scams and how to avoid them.

4. Trust your instincts – if something seems too good to be true, it probably is.

5. Stay informed and stay vigilant – the digital landscape is constantly evolving, so it's essential to stay updated on the latest trends and threats.

Chapter 16

How to Be
a Model Citizen

Oscar grew up in a large cosmopolitan city. He was the son of well-to-do parents so he had the privilege of attending the best schools, wearing fine clothes, being driven in luxury cars by private  chauffeurs, and attending parties to which only the rich and famous were invited. By his 20th birthday, he had visited about ten countries. He was heard uttering this response to a gentleman who solicited some form of assistance for the community from him: "Sorry, I am too busy. I have neither the time, desire, nor inclination for that sort of thing. My Dad pays enough taxes; let the government do it."

Less than a quarter of a mile from Oscar's mansion was Kenneth's family. This family, unlike Oscar's, had modest means. Kenneth walked to the neighborhood government primary school and later attended the nearest public secondary school. At a very young age, Kenneth was taught not to litter. At age 14, he organized a group of ten children to pick up paper bags, wrappings, and other such garbage from the sides of his street. Kenneth never travelled abroad but he was always an active member of his community, promoting and supporting sporting and other social events. At age 25, he was elected head of the Community Volunteer's Association.

Which of these two men would qualify as a good world citizen?

Having once been a teenager myself, I know that despite what people think, you do want to do your part to make the world a better place. How can you be a good citizen of this world and do great things for others?

Being a good citizen isn't about donning a cape and being Superman. It's about embracing kindness, staying informed, and making impactful choices. We'll explore the power of small acts, the joy of volunteering, and the magic of supporting local communities. Together, we will look at issues such as responsible online citizenship, eco-friendly living, and the importance of respecting diversity. From participating in democracy to practicing empathy, each chapter is a steppingstone toward becoming a well-rounded, informed, and compassionate global citizen. So, buckle up for an exciting journey as we look at ways to make a positive imprint on the world —the world is waiting for the incredible impact only you can make!

How to be a good citizen of this world

Being a good citizen of the world is all about contributing positively to the community, respecting others, and caring for the environment. Here are some simple yet impactful ways to be a good global citizen:

1. Practice Kindness

Practicing kindness is like spreading sunshine wherever you go. It's not just a nicety; it's a powerful tool to make the world a better place, especially for young people like you.

Start with simple acts. Hold the door open for someone, lend a helping hand, or flash a warm smile—these little gestures create a ripple effect of positivity. In a world that can sometimes feel chaotic, kindness is your superpower to make someone's day brighter.

Be a good listener. Sometimes, people just need someone to hear them out. Your genuine interest can make a significant difference. It's like giving a small piece of your heart to make someone else's day a bit lighter.

Embrace inclusivity. Reach out to those who might feel left out or lonely. Small acts of inclusion, such as inviting someone to join your group, can foster a sense of belonging and warmth.

Online or offline, treat others with respect. Cyber-kindness matters, too. Pause before posting, avoid harsh words, and remember there's a real person behind every screen.

Kindness isn't a one-time thing; make it a habit. Challenge yourself to do something kind every day. It could be as simple as leaving a positive note, offering a compliment, or volunteering your time.

In a world that sometimes feels too fast-paced, being kind slows things down. It connects us, reminds us of our shared humanity, and creates a world where everyone feels valued. So, go ahead, sprinkle kindness like confetti—the world could always use more of it!

2. Volunteering and giving back

Volunteering and giving back to your community are great ways to become a good citizen of the world. By offering your time and resources, you can help make a positive impact on the lives of others and contribute to the well-being of your community.

Find a cause that resonates with you. Choose an organization or issue that you care about, whether it's environmental conservation, education, or poverty alleviation. This will make your volunteering experience more enjoyable and fulfilling.

Research local opportunities: Look for volunteer opportunities in your area by searching online or contacting local nonprofit organizations. Many communities have volunteer centers that can help connect you with the right opportunities.

Be consistent: Regularly volunteering shows commitment and allows you to build relationships with the people you're helping and the other volunteers. Consistency also helps you develop new skills and knowledge about the issue you're addressing.

Encourage others to join: Share your experiences with friends and family and invite them to volunteer alongside you. This can help create a supportive network of volunteers and increase the impact of your efforts. Also, it's more fun to be engaging in helpful activities with people who you are close to.

Reflect on your experiences. Take time to think about the impact your volunteering has had on both yourself and the people you've helped. This can help you stay motivated and inspired to continue giving back.

3. Being an active member of the community is important

Becoming an active member of your community means participating in local events, attending meetings, and staying informed about issues affecting your community. This can help you develop a sense of belonging and foster a strong, supportive community.

Attend local events: Participate in community events, such as festivals, concerts, and sports games. This helps you meet your neighbors and learn about the interests and values of your community.

Join local organizations: Get involved in groups that focus on community improvement, such as neighborhood associations or parent-teacher organizations. These groups can help you stay informed about local issues and give you a platform to share your ideas and concerns.

Vote and stay informed: Participate in local elections and stay informed about issues affecting your community. This helps ensure that your voice is heard and that your community's needs are addressed.

Support local businesses: shop at local businesses, attend local farmers' markets, and dine at local restaurants. This helps support your community's economy and fosters a sense of unity among residents.

Engage in dialogue: Talk to your neighbors and fellow community members about the issues affecting your community. This can help you build relationships and work together to find solutions.

4. Educate Others

Educating others is a super cool way to share knowledge, spark curiosity, and make a positive impact on the world around you. Whether it's enlightening someone on a topic you're passionate about or helping him or her see a different perspective, being an educator in your own way is a fantastic contribution.

Start with conversations. Share interesting facts, engage in discussions, and encourage an open exchange of ideas. A simple chat can be a powerful tool for expanding someone's understanding.

Use your social media powers for good. Share insightful articles, documentaries, or even your own thoughts on subjects that matter. Social platforms aren't just for selfies; they're awesome spaces to spread awareness and knowledge.

Be patient and approachable. Not everyone has the same level of knowledge about every topic, so be understanding and ready to answer questions without judgment. Your approach can make learning fun and engaging.

Share your experiences. Personal stories are captivating and relatable. Whether it's a book you loved, a volunteer experience that touched your heart, or a lesson you learned, your stories can inspire and educate.

Lead by example. If you're passionate about a cause, show others how they can get involved too. Whether it's volunteering, supporting a local initiative, or adopting sustainable practices, your actions speak volumes.

Remember, you don't need a classroom to be an educator. Every conversation, post or interaction is an opportunity to share knowledge. By educating others, you're not just spreading information; you're igniting a spark that can lead to positive change. Keep rocking that wisdom!

Embracing Causes

Embracing causes is like wrapping your arms around the issues that tug at your heartstrings. It's about diving headfirst into what you're passionate about and turning that passion into positive action. Embracing causes that matter to you is another way to be a good citizen of the world. By supporting these causes, you can help raise awareness and create positive change.

1. Educate yourself: Learn about the issues you care about, and stay informed about the latest news and developments. This will help you make informed decisions about how to support these causes.

2. Advocate for change: Use your voice to speak up for the causes you care about. This can include writing letters to politicians, attending rallies, or sharing information on social media.

3. Donate: Support organizations working on the issues you care about by making financial contributions. Even small donations can make a big difference.

4. Use your skills and talents: Offer your unique skills and talents to support the causes you care about. This can include volunteering your graphic design skills for a nonprofit or using your writing skills to raise awareness about an issue.

5. Encourage others to support the cause: Share information about the causes you care about with your friends, family, and social networks. This can help raise awareness and inspire others to get involved.

In conclusion, being a good citizen of the world involves volunteering, giving back, being an active member of the community, and embracing causes. By following these steps and staying committed to making a positive impact, you can help create a better world for everyone.

Extra Credit: 5 Things to Remember

1. Being a good citizen is about embracing kindness, staying informed, and making impactful choices.
2. Be a good listener, sometimes people just need someone to hear them out.
3. One fulfilling way of giving back is volunteering and giving by finding a cause that resonates with you.
4. Share your experiences, personal stories are captivating and relatable.
5. Be an advocate for change.

CONCLUSION

As you reach the final pages of this book, I hope you're filled with a newfound sense of confidence, empowerment, and excitement for the journey ahead. You've embarked on a transformative journey of self-discovery and growth, diving into the depths of essential life skills, social dynamics, and practical wisdom that will serve as your compass in the years to come.

Remember, the lessons you've learned within these pages are not merely words on a page—they're the building blocks of your future success and happiness. I hope you feel equipped with the tools you need to thrive.

As you step out into the world, I encourage you to embrace each new experience as an opportunity for growth, learning, and personal development.

Keep an open mind, stay curious, and never stop striving to be the best version of yourself. Above all, remember that you are capable, resilient, and infinitely deserving of all the love, success, and happiness that life has to offer. Trust in yourself, follow your passions, and never lose sight of the incredible potential that lies within you.

As you turn the final page and embark on the next chapter of your journey, know that you carry with you the wisdom, knowledge, and strength to create a life that's as extraordinary as you are. Here's to a future filled with endless possibilities, boundless opportunities, and infinite joy. Congratulations on completing this book, and may your path be brightened by the light of your own brilliance. Go forth and shine brightly, my friend. The world is waiting for you.

ABOUT THE AUTHOR

Koren Norton is an author, counselor, and workplace consultant who lives in Antigua & Barbuda, West Indies. Her passion is helping people to be happy, fulfilled, and successful. She enjoys writing, making lists, traveling, reading, eating tasty foods, listening to music, playing games solving puzzles, and spending quality time with her family. Love is her favorite thing in the world! Koren finds inspiration in talking to her clients and spending time at the beach and she always focuses on the positive side of life. She can be contacted at koren@consultkoren.com.

Other Books by Koren Norton

- On Becoming a Fulfilled Woman
- You can do it: Your Personal Guide to Successful Living
- Now do it: A 52-week Guided Journal for Achieving Personal Success
- Retirement Planning, with Elijah James
- Tell it Like it is: The Scoop on Life and Lessons from a Brother and Sister, with Kelvin Grannum
- The Successful Woman Daily Planner
- The Successful Entrepreneur Daily Planner
- Remembering Paradise: A Journal and Activity Book on Antigua & Barbuda
- Effective Succession Planning, with Elijah James
- Ask Koren: 101 Responses to Your Most Important Questions
- Winning at Work: A Guided Workbook for Thriving in Your Career with Confidence and Flair
- From Hurt to Healing: A Journal for Persons Recovering From a Toxic Relationship
- Love Untangled: Unlocking the good, bad, ugly and awkward sides of relationships
- Mindful Moments: A Puzzle and Activity Book for Adults Celebrating Life

Website: www.consultkoren.com
Facebook & Instagram: consultkoren268
App Store: AskKoren

9 798869 318008